Previous Praise...

"Eerie and thoroughly engrossing. The haunting world of Natalie Glasgow lures you into the shroud of the unknown and won't let go. I couldn't put it down!" – K.P. Kulski, author of *Fairest Flesh*

"[Piper's] fiction is remarkable in its range" – *Esquire*

"Downright chilling. Every page is as dread-inducing as a creaking footstep in an empty house. These linked stories of hauntings and possessions are exceptional in their imagination, and with compelling characters, sharp prose, and swift pacing, this collection has all the makings of a horror classic. Hailey Piper is a remarkable talent." – Rachel Harrison, USA Today Bestselling author of *Cackle* and *Black Sheep*

"This is a masterpiece." – Laurel Hightower, This Is Horror Award-winning author of *Crossroads*

"Nothing like anything I have read before and it had me absolutely hooked." – P.L. McMillan, author of *What Remains When the Stars Burn Out*

"Truly original" – Sara Tantlinger, Bram Stoker Award-winning author of *The Devil's Dreamland* "exquisite, lovely" – Gwendolyn Kiste, Lambda Award-winning author of *Reluctant Immortals*

"There comes a point when you think you've seen it all. What a lovely surprise..." – V. Castro, Bram Stoker Award-nominated author of *Goddess of Filth*

"Poignant and shocking and bordering on the mythic" – Joe Koch, Shirley Jackson Award-nominated author of *The Couvade*

"Mysterious and strange" – Sadie Hartmann, Bram Stoker Award-nominated author of *101 Horror Books to Read Before You're Murdered*

"One of the most original possession tales I have read. Ever." – Steve Stred, Splatterpunk Award-nominated author of *Mastodon*

"excellent and unique" – J.A.W. McCarthy, Shirley Jackson Award-nominated author of *Sleep Alone*

"truly terrifying and tense" – Brennan LaFaro, author of *Slattery Falls*

"executed beautifully, not a word wasted" – Red Lagoe, author of *Lucid Screams*

<u>**OTHER BOOKS BY HAILEY PIPER**</u>

<u>**Standalone**</u>
Queen of Teeth
A Light Most Hateful
Cruel Angels Past Sundown
Your Mind Is a Terrible Thing
Unfortunate Elements of My Anatomy
Cranberry Cove
No Gods for Drowning

<u>**The Worm and His Kings series**</u>
The Worm and His Kings
Even the Worm Will Turn
Song of the Tyrant Worm

To J,
Wife, witch, and wonder.

HAILEY PIPER

Published by Strangehouse Books

an imprint of Rooster Republic Press LLC

www.roosterrepublicpress.com

roosterrepublicpress@gmail.com

Cover Design, Interior, and Illustrations by Nicholas Day and Don Noble

ISBN: 978-1-946335-54-8

Printed in the USA

Find our catalog at

www.roosterrepublicpress.com

Contents

GLASS HOUSE

Connecticut, November 1978

Heather Glasgow sucked in a startled breath, heart leaping up her throat, and the freshly washed drinking glass shattered across the off-white kitchen floor tiles. She had only left the thin fluorescent light on above the sink to wash the dishes. Now she turned around and faced the kitchen's entrance, where the stairway light crossing the living room backlit a narrow figure.

"Natalie," Heather said, touching a hand to her chest. Her yellow dish glove soaked sudsy water into her sweater. "You startled me."

"I'm sorry," Natalie said. Her voice was a squeaky mouse between the kitchen and the living room.

"It's not your fault."

Heather had been lost in her own thoughts, and Nathaniel had remodeled the stairs too well last year. Their steps hardly gave a sound even when he went stomping up in his boots, let alone when ten-year-old Natalie—no, eleven now, she'd turned eleven last month—descended the stairs in fluffy purple pajamas and pink bunny slippers. Heather hadn't even registered Natalie's question, the one that had startled her, until right now.

When's Daddy coming home?

Instead of answering, she grabbed the broom and dustpan from beside the humming refrigerator.

"I can help," Natalie said.

"I have it." Heather sighed through her nose. She needed to do better not being short with Natalie. It wasn't her fault, remember? She had no reason to think her mother would startle so easily or had any dark thoughts to lose herself in.

One soft slipper crossed the kitchen's threshold. "But Mom—"

Heather let the dustpan clack against the floor. "Sweetheart, there's broken glass."

This stopped Natalie. She slid back a step onto the living room carpet and waited, her wide eyes dark and doll-like against her pale face in the gloom.

"Get to bed," Heather said, gentler now. "I'll come say good night when I'm finished here."

Natalie stared for a long moment, her startling question unanswered, and then sulked away. "Okay, Mom."

Heather watched Natalie cross the living room and climb the stairs, silent as she'd come except for her hand making a *shush* noise as it slid up the banister. She disappeared onto the second floor, and Heather waited to hear creaking door hinges before she started on sweeping up the glass.

When had she become *Mom* instead of *Mommy*? And why had Nathaniel remained *Daddy*? These were questions she would have asked Nathaniel were he here, watching her sweep shards and glass bits into the dustpan. He might've told her the change would've been reversed had they had a boy.

"But we have a little girl," Heather whispered. "And she keeps asking for you."

No one responded. That had been the way of the house for three nights now, since that run back and forth from the hospital. It had all been so sudden—chest pains in the house, an ambulance ride, an overnight stay for observation.

And then gone in his sleep. Heather couldn't blame herself for coming home, looking at ponderous Natalie, and then blurting out that *Daddy* was feeling better, so good that he'd taken another of his trips out of the country. Yes, all of a sudden. Yes, without saying goodbye.

It was either tell a lie or break down in that moment like the piece-of-shit drinking glass Heather was now tapping into the kitchen's tall garbage bin. Pretending had made that first night easier, but nothing had been easy since.

She wasn't sure how many more instances of weathering that question—*When's Daddy coming home?*—she had left in her.

The ceiling *thumped*. Not above the kitchen. It sounded like it had come from above Nathaniel's study, meaning Natalie hadn't climbed into bed. She was waiting for her good night from Mom and would keep herself occupied until she got it. Likely she'd opened up her little desk to pull out paper and markers or crayons, and she would go drawing whichever animals she planned to dream about until the art was ready for her bedroom walls. She had more animals surrounding her than her father's study.

Eleven years old, and yet still a child in too many ways.

Heather dove her gloved hands into the sink and hurried through the last of the dishes. She had let them pile these past couple of days. She would finish this, and then say good night to Natalie, and then get herself to bed, and her sister Alicia would call again soon to ask for the phone numbers for Nathaniel's friends and colleagues, and Heather would have to visit the funeral home tomorrow, and what would she tell Natalie then?

When's Daddy coming home?

Heather wanted the answer to be *Now, right now*. She stroked a sponge down the last plate and waited for Nathaniel to close his burly hands around her waist, for his breath to brush her ear before he kissed her neck.

She could almost feel him.

But when she looked down at her middle, there was only her sweater, now slightly damp with dishwater. If any hands would hold her now, they belonged to the no one who would take Nathaniel's place in the Glasgow house. No one in his favorite chair. No one in his study.

Happy family, strong family, he would always say.

What did that make Heather and Natalie in this time of destructive misery? Were they weak? Would they *always* be weak?

Heather rinsed the last dish and set it in the steel drying rack. Clear droplets snaked toward a bubbly corner where she could have done a better job running the plate under the faucet. There were a lot of things she could be doing better. In the house. For herself.

For her daughter. How was she supposed to do any of this alone?

She stripped off the yellow dish gloves, and their wet smack against the sink basin reminded her of Nathaniel dragging damp boots into the house. A pain in the ass, but it would never happen again. The no one would not wear boots, would not plant them in puddles, and would not forget to wipe them on the welcome mat outside.

Another *thump* sounded from above. Heather crossed the living room and started up the stairs. They were silent beneath her, too. Like mother, like daughter.

She peered over the banister at the dark furniture and then the closed double doors to Nathaniel's study. Part of her wanted to disbelieve that night at the hospital and choose a faith in opening those doors. Wasn't it easier to believe that he was in there, right now? If she could reach out for those doors, the air inside would touch her like his fingers.

Except that study belonged to no one now. The same no one who would sit with Heather when Natalie eventually graduated from high school. The no one who would give her away at her wedding. There would be no one else to understand the grandparental awe of seeing their child have her own child someday.

No future, no now, only the past. Heather thought of rough footsteps and a temper in the air when Nathaniel would come home inebriated from a trip abroad, and she wished the lie she told Natalie could be true.

She would have taken an angry husband any night over this relentless no one.

At the top of the stairs, she passed her bedroom door and made for Natalie's. The hall stretched like a slumbering beast, holding still in its sleep so as not to warn a predator of easy prey. Natalie wouldn't even know anyone was coming. Heather could startle her with a question, too, but was that the kind of relationship she wanted to have when they were only a family of two now?

Less than that, she could stay silent in the hall, as if Natalie's mother had gone to the emptiness, same as her father. Wouldn't that be easier? It would become no one's responsibility to tell Natalie the truth, and Heather could puff away in the November wind.

She smiled to herself. She used to think she was a good mother, but put to the test, she couldn't be sure anymore.

Didn't she owe it to Natalie to try?

Heather raised her fist and let it hover outside the bedroom door. A quiet tune danced through the wood, the sound of Natalie humming to herself. Yes, she had to be drawing. Not a care in the world right now except for missing her father. Such a child, but maybe that was a blessing. Heather should appreciate it before it disappeared. To knock on this door, open it, and tell the truth might crush that childhood forever.

In fact, Heather was certain of it. Because the no one at the core of her misery could never be as simple an absence as if Nathaniel had never existed. This wasn't like he'd left her for another woman—God, that would be a different problem. At least then Natalie would still have a father.

But instead, they had this life, and this night, and Heather needed to answer Natalie's crucial question for herself before she knocked on her daughter's bedroom door, and opened it, and let the night shatter like a drinking glass against the kitchen floor.

When's Daddy coming home?

"Never," Heather whispered, her throat tightening. "Never, never, never."

THE WRONG SIDE OF THE NIGHT

December 1978

Grief could fall in the dust when it wasn't yours. It would get back up again, sure as Alicia Meadows would pull into her sister's driveway on her return trip, but right now she sat behind the wheel of her Camaro, the air held that will-snow-soon crispness as it wafted past her windows along Route 29, and the radio was playing The Doors.

And most importantly, she was leaving the grief behind. She couldn't stay at Heather's house a minute longer, and going home would be like abandoning family, but heading out to pick up post-Christmas candy for her niece, Natalie? Alicia could take this excuse—this errand. The grief would still be waiting in Heather's house. In Natalie's room.

A few of that little girl's light brown hairs swayed from Alicia's sweater, clinging, *reminding*, trying to point like accusatory boneless fingers.

"No, no, don't do that to me," Alicia said. "A few minutes of peace, that's all I want."

She cranked up the radio as the darkness deepened around her headlights. Skeletal trees swept past the winding asphalt, and road signs came and went to the song's rhythm as it came to a close, Alicia bobbing her head and beating her palm against the steering wheel as she shouted alongside Jim Morrison.

Until something beneath her Camaro's hood gave a throaty gasp. She'd never heard a car make a noise like that.

But she recognized what came next—an uneasy rumble, and the little *tick* of the check engine light going on, and the uneasy quiet seeping in as her car became a ghost in the night.

"No, no," she said, petting the dashboard. "Come on, baby, I'm good to you."

The car didn't care. She could only grip the steering wheel and force her Camaro to the side of the road, where it coasted to a jittering stop. She hurried the keys out of the ignition, and herself out of the car, and gave it a wide berth along Route 29's shoulder in case smoke began to belch from the hood.

But nothing happened. The car lay dead and dark in the winter cold.

Alicia returned to grab her purse, but she didn't hang around. That first noise had been too weird, and if her Camaro planned to explode, she didn't want to find herself standing anywhere near it.

Her gaze trailed the near-total darkness. There were no streetlights on this stretch of Route 29, and only a sliver of moonlight lit the sky. Alicia couldn't remember if it was supposed to be waxing or waning. If she lingered another few nights, maybe the light would get better. Or it would get worse, blackened by the new moon, meanwhile she couldn't survive out here waiting to see. The next patch of town lay past a few miles of slopes and turns, and the road wasn't going to walk itself.

Alicia's breath clouded through her lips. "Serves me damn right."

She put one boot ahead of the other for a few paces and then stopped to fish in her purse for her lighter and a cigarette. Heather never let Alicia smoke in her house, under decree of her now-late husband, and Alicia had said she was trying to quit, but she needed a small mercy right now.

Golden luminance spilled her shadow ahead as she plucked up her plastic lighter. She spun on one heel and faced the growing light—no, *lights*, the high beams of a slender sedan approaching over the sloping asphalt.

Between the sisters, Heather might have grabbed up all the severity, what she'd call maturity, but Alicia had the sense. She knew to be wary of what she didn't know. And she knew two golden bad ideas when she saw them.

But the hike to town would be long and cold. She'd be lucky to make it before two in the morning and without pneumonia or worse. And the woods stretched thick to either side of the road. Anything could lunge out of them before she reached a phone booth or gas station.

She slid her lighter back into her purse and stuck out her thumb.

The sedan eased alongside her. Its inside light flashed alive on a square-jawed man in his mid-thirties with a friendly smile and the right amount of stubble on his winter-paled face to look rugged but not sloppy. A brown coat hid his outstretched arm as he rolled down the passenger's side window.

"Going my way?" he asked, buttery smooth.

What did he see through his window? Alicia Meadows, dark-haired and wild-eyed, a little older than him, dressed in a crimson sweater and jeans like she needed a night by the fireplace rather than walking the road.

"I'm a big fan of civilization," Alicia said.

The door popped open, and the driver beckoned her inside. She nestled onto beaten leather seating, shut the door, and slung her seatbelt on.

"It's pretty close," she said. "A few miles up the road."

"I'll have you there in a jiffy," the driver said, but he didn't look at her when he spoke. His eyes locked ahead as if there were some animal in the road she couldn't see.

The car lurched forward and resumed its ride up Route 29. Alicia hugged her chest, one hand curled into a fist. She was trembling with cold—or was that anticipation of this ride going wrong? She'd never hitchhiked before, not even when she was too young or carless to drive.

"You cold?" the driver asked, finally glancing her way.

"Forgot my coat in my car," she said.

Still going forty-five miles per hour and climbing, the driver reached behind Alicia's seat. She braced herself again for that moment of imminent wrong, when he might jab a knife through the seat or some other nightmare she'd probably plucked up from a bad movie.

He instead emerged with a thin autumn jacket, its chest black, its sleeves turquoise. "It isn't much, but with your sweater, it should get you warmed up, right as rain."

Alicia thanked him and slipped it on. She hadn't realized how cold she was until sliding her sweatered arms inside. The jacket was a warm hug made manifest in fabric. Like it had been lying on the floor of the car only waiting for someone to need it again.

"A gentleman," Alicia said, smirking. "Lucky me."

"Yes." Oncoming lights gleamed in the driver's teeth. "Lucky you to break down in wintertime."

"Could be worse." Alicia shrugged against the jacket, and its sleeves made a *swish-swish* sound as she settled. "It's not like you grow up thinking your car's apt to crap out on you."

"You don't grow up dreaming about a no-problems car either," the driver said. "Nobody dreams of it going wrong until it happens. We just assume a perfect life is coming, any day now, if you want it bad enough. They say you can do anything when you grow up." He glanced again at Alicia. "Why do they tell kids that? Saying they can be anything they want when they grow up? It ain't true. They don't even know if you'll get to grow up."

Alicia bobbed her head as if this radio were blasting The Doors too. "Yeah, it's pretty fucked."

They rode in silence for the few minutes it took to reach an Exxon station. The driver idled at the lot's edge as Alicia stepped out and then wished her good night and good luck. She waved as he sped away. No odd looks, no touching, didn't even offer his name or ask hers.

"What a weirdo," Alicia muttered. But the good kind, she supposed.

She turned from the road and approached the gas station, weighing whether to ask if they had a tow, or a phone, her purse-free arm going *swish-swish* at her side.

The jacket. She was still wearing it.

She looked to Route 29, hoping the driver had realized and turned around, but distance had eaten his taillights. There was no sign of him.

She closed a fist around the jacket's hem. It hadn't exactly come with a phone number or address stitched into the material. She would have to hang onto it, at least for a while, in case she saw the driver again someday. In case its true owner wanted it back.

The dream hit Alicia a week later, close to New Year's. She didn't know it was a dream at first, as always. It only told on itself at the end, and that was the part she could remember, of driving her sharp fingernails into her abdomen's soft flesh. Piercing, pulling, stretching herself open into the birthing of a stranger inside her. No smell climbed from within, no acrid taste in the air. There was only this gaping hole.

And someone peering from inside it.

She blinked awake with a blanket encircling half her face. Had she been inside herself in the dream, looking out? Did that symbolize pregnancy?

Swish-swish.

Alicia sat up from her pillows. The room hung dark and cold around her. She usually turned the heat down at night, saving on the gas bill for her tiny house, but the clawing air said the heat might have shut off entirely. A busted furnace was all she needed after paying for the Camaro's tow and diagnostic only to learn the car was perfectly fine.

Swish-swish.

The sudden noise cast a shudder through her. Wasn't that the sound the jacket had made when she wore it that one night?

She glanced around her room, trying to remember if she'd tossed it in here, but no, she'd left in the foyer, hanging from a wall hook beside her winter coats. Maybe she'd left the front door open, and the wind was blowing the jacket against the wall. *Swish-swish*, it would go. That would explain the house's chill, too.

Her feet slid into thin slippers and carried her to the bedroom doorway. The rest of the house was a blue-black soup. She reached for the nearest wall switch, ready to light up the living room enough to walk toward the standing lamp.

But the foyer lingered in view of the bedroom door, the curse of a tiny house, and she could make out the shape of the jacket from here. It did not look to be hanging from a hook beside her coats. And it didn't sway with an open-door breeze—the front door was shut.

The jacket instead stretched beyond its collar, as if it had grown a round head, and its hem rained down the wall toward the floor in the suggestion of hips and legs. Even its surface looked too smooth to be crumpled from a hook. The chest and sleeves stretched around the shape of someone wearing it.

Alicia's finger hovered over the light switch, but she didn't want to flick it on anymore. If she was wrong, fantastic. But if she was right, and someone somehow wore the jacket while it hung from the wall, she wouldn't want to know that. She would wish she was still dreaming.

Swish-swish.

A panicked yelp shot up her throat, and she slammed the bedroom door shut and locked it. Her back squeezed against the wood, waiting for another sound, another suggestion of shape.

There was nothing. The night held quiet with winter until morning, when Alicia awoke crumpled on the floor.

She found the jacket hanging from its hook, exactly as she'd left it.

"Obviously I know there was nobody there," Alicia said, a shrug in her voice. "This is just some super-neurotic, psychopathic, ticking time bomb, biological clock, ghost-baby bullshit episode. I bet it runs in the family. Small wonder Heather's handling the death of her husband so badly. And you should meet our mother."

"I've barely met you yourself, Alicia," Dennis said. "Let's take a step back."

He sat in a dull blue seat at the center of his office, clutching a clipboard to his navy blue button-up. Framed paintings adorned the walls with ships at sea and peaceful mountains, each whispering for Alicia to relax so intensely that her nerves were on fire. She would've done better had each been a painting of the word *PANIC* over and over. The bookshelves carried dull-looking spines and an out-facing spiralbound yellow cover reading *Diagnostic and Statistical Manual: Mental Disorders.*

Alicia had seen everything clearly when she came in. The room now looked askew from where she lay across the off-yellow couch. She didn't need to lie down, but the little newspaper cartoons always showed psychiatric clients lying on a couch. It wasn't as comforting or cartoonish as she'd hoped.

She sat up to look Dennis in the eye. "Come on, doc, you got to help me. I'm your desperate patient."

Dennis gave a wry smile. "I'm not a doctor, Alicia, I'm a licensed counselor. Which makes you my client. And a first session is more about getting to know you than smoothing out any wrinkles in your life. I can't help unless we take our time."

"Oh, sure you can. I got most people figured out within ten minutes." Alicia reached for the nearest end table, where she plucked her half-smoldered cigarette from the crook of a black ashtray. "So, what is it? Spending too much time with my niece? My uterus saying, *You want one, you better bake one?* I'm not getting the message."

"That could explain the dream," Dennis said, tapping his clipboard. "Motherhood is a common step in the path of your life's completion."

Alicia twitched as she sucked at her cigarette. Dennis sounded like one of those life-as-a-set-of-boxes types. Less than ten minutes here and she had him sorted.

"But your encounter in the night," he went on. "You aren't being haunted, Alicia. And it very well might have to do with your spending time at your sister's house."

Alicia tittered. "What, I'm grieving Nathaniel? I barely knew the guy. And he never made a damn effort to change that. At her bridal shower, we called him the Lion. Not because he was fierce or anything, but because lionesses do the real work while a lion claims the pride, and that's what I saw coming for my sister. Lazy Lion Nathaniel, Hardworking Heather. Never mind her money troubles now, but he wasn't a star husband. Sincerely, I don't miss the guy enough for nightmares. My mess is something else."

Dennis flashed another smile. "Consider which is more likely—the worlds of the living and the dead crossing paths because you accidentally kept a borrowed jacket, or that you've taken on some of your sister's grief? A grief she doesn't sound like she's handling very well. That would explain why she's leaning on you to take a dominant role with herself and her daughter."

"Wow. Consider me truly mystified." Alicia crushed her cigarette into the ashtray and started up from the couch. "No disrespect, doc, but I think I need a second opinion. A more open mind to whatever the hell's wrong with me. Any recommendations?"

Dennis leaned back in his seat. "I know other counselors, even psychologists," he said. "But if you're dead-set on birthing and ghosts—"

"I'm not set on ghosts."

"Strange happenstance, then." Dennis tore off a sliver of paper from the edge of his clipboard. "I have a client, a troubled young woman—I won't get into her personal business, that would violate her client rights, but she knows a midwife who's also something of an occult curiosity."

"Occult?" Alicia asked. "Like what, a witch?"

"Isn't that what you want?" Dennis flipped through a rolodex on his middle bookshelf, plucked up a card, and scribbled onto his torn paper. "I'll send you to whomever you'd like to talk to."

"Is that important?" Alicia asked, taking the paper. "Who I'd like to talk to?"

"Of course," Dennis said. "That's the point of any counsel. Someone you'll open up to. It's the same whether it's a counselor, a lawyer, a doctor, a real estate agent like yourself, or a so-called witch." He tapped the paper. "You want to talk to Margaret Willow."

Alicia did not want to talk to Margaret Willow. She wanted to get on with her life. She wanted to crawl out of this wet hole she'd found herself hunched in. Its sides were caving beneath her palms as she climbed, fingers sinking into soppy muck. And when she emerged from the hole into a chilly rain, she wanted to sink her teeth into its ragged, meaty edges and pull and pluck and—

She started awake and thrashed to one side, turning on the bedside lamp. It cast a calm golden glow through its lampshade across her bed, and she studied her hands for soil or worse.

There was nothing. Her fingernails were immaculate.

Swish-swish.

Something soft hit her bedroom door. She thrust back against the headboard, shoulders raised, legs curled to her belly. A minute dragged by in almost silence. Was there another *swish*? Some different sound? She couldn't tell, could only guess while her lavender walls and soft bedspread took on a hostile atmosphere.

When she finally pried herself from the bed and opened the bedroom door, she found the jacket crumpled on the floor inches from her slippers. The turquoise sleeves were damp with cold droplets. It smelled like rain.

The phone rang three times before it clicked, and a woman with a gentle English accent spoke into Alicia's ear.

"May I ask who's calling?"

"Yeah, I'm Alicia Meadows. Got a tip to look for Margaret Willow. This her?"

"No," the woman said.

"Her secretary?" Alicia asked.

"No," the woman said again, terser now. "But she's coming out of the bathroom. One moment."

Alicia waited, the phone pressed against her head. The light of mid-morning pressed bright thumbs against her eyes, and she turned to face the wall, letting her free hand cup the phone, and then letting her fingers descend the twirling cord toward the receiver in a nervous dance. Nothing felt right about making this call, and the strangeness was sapping her confidence.

Or maybe the woman who answered next had stolen it. She sounded official, even stern, and probably Midwestern.

"This is Margaret."

Alicia sucked in a harsh breath. She could do this. "Hi there, Margaret. Can you do a favor after this and apologize to the Brit for me? Think I insulted her."

"I'll try," Margaret said. "I have to warn you, Ms. Meadows, I'm full up on clients right now."

"Didn't know that happened with midwives." Alicia pincered her hands around the telephone cord—she needed to rein herself in or else she might piss off someone who could help her. "But I guess you got to be ready whenever, wherever."

"That's right."

"This isn't about babies though," Alicia said. "At least, I hope it isn't. I woke up from what I think was a pregnancy dream, and—"

Her teeth sank into her lower lip. She didn't want to say *ghost* again. She couldn't remember how many times she'd said it since that first night with the jacket, and to say it one more time felt like summoning Bloody Mary through a mirror when she was a kid, only this time the ghost might genuinely rush through the dark and tear her away.

"And?" Margaret asked.

Alicia eased her teeth from her lip. "There was someone in my house who wasn't there."

The conversation turned one-sided as Alicia rambled out the story, starting with Heather and Natalie, Alicia's need to get away—hoping Margaret wouldn't jump to the counselor's conclusions—Alicia's car breaking down, her catching a lift, the jacket first coming to her, the peaceful nights until she began staying at her house again, and the unpeaceful, jacket-filled nights that began shortly after.

By evening, they were on the road. Alicia had pulled her Camaro to the same Exxon station where she'd first realized the jacket remained draped around her. It had felt so warm that night, but maybe that was an illusion. Or maybe it hadn't chosen her yet.

She still had it now, folded in the passenger's seat beside her. They waited together without so much as a *swish* until another car pulled up to Alicia's rear and beeped the horn twice, Margaret's signal of *Yes, it's me, now lead*.

And Alicia obeyed.

Their caravan of two coasted out of the gas station and down Route 29. Alicia didn't want her car to rumble and choke again, growing superstitious of this road in the winter evening, but Margaret had given clear instructions. The lack of explanation for its breakdown made that night all the more suspicious, and Alicia wondered if it was somehow the jacket's doing, calling to her from its owner's car.

She doubted that was a mystery Margaret Willow could solve. Alicia would be happy enough if the haunting would end.

Winter daylight eased from the world, casting the forested road with enough darkness to look almost familiar against that December night. Almost right. Where the turns and slopes seemed most inviting, Alicia made a U-turn and pulled her Camaro to the shoulder.

Margaret parked behind her and stepped out. She was a brick of a lady in her mid-forties, a few inches shorter than Alicia. Her hair hung at her shoulders, and she wore a puffy winter coat that hid most of her outfit. The last red sunlight glinted in the spectacles perched above her round cheeks.

"Is this where you broke down that night?" she asked.

"Taking my best shot. It was dark out." Alicia gazed up at the sky and hugged her coat around her. "Getting dark now, too."

"Maybe it's this side then. We'll try the trees." Margaret pulled a slender black flashlight from one of her coat pockets and started off the road, toward the skeletal-treed woods. "And bring the jacket."

Alicia fetched it from the car. Its swishy fabric was cold against her fingers as if she'd let it fly flaglike from the car window rather than having kept it toasty beside her. Had it ever been warm since she first put it on?

She hurried to follow off the road. "You planning to tell me what we're supposed to be doing out here?"

Margaret switched on her flashlight and aimed it at the trees. "If I explain it to you, it might frighten you, and I need you to listen to me."

"You're kind of frightening me anyhow," Alicia muttered. She caught up at Margaret's heels. "How come you don't ask me why I didn't throw the jacket away? Or burn it? I must look like some maniac, clinging to this thing."

"That wouldn't help," Margaret said. "I think you knew that already. And besides, if you left it, you'd wonder if it was going to find you again. I assume you'd like to put this all to rest instead."

Alicia hesitated at the edge of Route 29. She knew enough to know what she didn't know, but did she know enough to leave that knowledge alone when it didn't belong to her? Her gaze drifted to the jacket in her arms. Couldn't she let it flop onto the roadside here? Why the hell had she kept it?

To return it to its true owner. That kindly driver might pull up alongside her again someday, and she didn't want to tell him to his handsome face that she'd thrown his gift in the mud or burned it in a parking lot.

But there was something else to it. Something in the woods.

White trees slid around them as Route 29 faded away, and the fingertips of their limbs burrowed into the blackened sky. Dry leaves and sticks littered the earth, and the absence of snow felt wrong for this time of year. Or perhaps the dark woods would have shrugged off its white intrusion.

The only relief from the night was Margaret's silhouette and her cone of golden radiance, aiming between the trees to light their way.

Alicia's breath came cloudy as she spoke. "I don't know what we're doing out here, but I'm at the edge of regretting this. Can we turn back?"

"Absolutely not." A sharpness took Margaret's voice. "If you turn back now, you'll regret it more than starting this."

Alicia licked her lips. She could swing around right now and reach the road in ten minutes. Her eyes winced at sudden brightness before she could start off—Margaret had wheeled around with her flashlight. A firm hand grasped Alicia's wrist.

"Take the end of the jacket's sleeve, the way I have your arm now," Margaret said. "And walk while leading it along, like you're guiding your niece."

"She's too old for that," Alicia said. She sounded more unfazed than she really felt.

"Drag it behind you." Margaret leaned close, and her breath puffed beneath Alicia's chin. "And above all else, do not *look* behind you. Do you understand?"

Alicia swallowed hard and nodded until Margaret seemed appeased. She turned again and resumed their forested walk, and Alicia's jacket-holding hand slid down to her thigh. The jacket dragged behind her as instructed, making drawn-out *swiiish* sounds against fallen branches and frozen leaves. Every step crackled as if the forest floor were matted in baby teeth breaking under Alicia's boots, and when Margaret's flashlight swept away, maybe the teeth were true in the dark.

A cigarette would be a dream right now. Something to burn and give Alicia a fragment of comfort against the cold.

She guessed that Margaret wouldn't approve of the distraction. They were wandering into lands unknown, populated by mysteries and ghosts. Such enigmatic territories could somehow crop up in the woods of Connecticut in the modern day, and Alicia had traipsed into them of her own free will.

"I'm letting you put me in danger, aren't I?" Alicia asked.

"Only if you don't listen." Margaret swept her flashlight beam in a searching arc ahead. "Whatever you've found, it hasn't crawled inside you. Unless I'm talking to it right now. Are you still you?"

Alicia was almost relieved. Not pregnant. But maybe she had something worse. "I'm still me."

"Do as I instruct and we'll keep it that way," Margaret said.

She reached into her coat and sprinkled a mix of crushed plant and soil onto the snowless ground. The green looked too vibrant for the season. Alicia almost turned to watch it behind her, but Margaret had instructed not to look. No messing this up—Alicia wanted to remain herself when this was over, if there was any self to be.

Even the trees didn't seem to know themselves. They were getting strange with their high limbs fading above, and only a silence seemed to drift down in return. The woods were always quiet in winter, the cold being a sound-killer, but it felt more like hands covering Alicia's ears, not wanting her to hear anything except the jacket behind her, sliding over the earth.

A branch snapped ahead. Alicia glanced to Margaret's left, where the edge of her flashlight beam's arc caught a shadow sliding around a tree trunk, there and then gone.

"What the hell was that?" Alicia snapped.

"Don't look behind you," Margaret said again. "To the side is fine, but never behind you."

Alicia forced her next step, and her next. One boot ahead of the other, same as that night on Route 29.

Except she'd never had to make any real journey. Not on foot. Maybe some other kind of journey then, one she hadn't agreed to when she left her sister's house, abandoning grief-paralyzed Heather Glasgow, and poor little Natalie Glasgow, and fair-weather Aunt Alicia had been paying for her selfishness since. She had offered Heather a shoulder to cry on and another set of hands to care for her daughter. Hell, she'd bitten her tongue that Heather wasn't much worse off. When had Nathaniel really helped around the house or spent decent time with his family? Always swelling his bank account on investments and then wandering abroad without wife or daughter, the Lion roaming Europe and Africa like he was the real thing and then bellowing through the home upon his return.

Heather could do better, and Alicia hadn't said it. She should be nominated for sainthood for that.

But maybe she could have done better herself. She could've urged Heather to get out of the house, coaxed her into a shopping trip, spent more time with Natalie. And she shouldn't have gone driving up Route 29 on that needless errand.

That excuse.

It had been the holidays. How could she judge dead Nathaniel Glasgow if she'd ditched the same two people in the same miserable house?

No rugged driver would come rolling through these woods on rescue tonight. There was only stern Margaret, her flaking weeds, and trembling Alicia behind her.

That quieting pressure lingered at her ears. She tried fixating on existing sounds when the night hid everything else. Margaret's footsteps. Alicia's footsteps. Her breath. The jacket making its *swiiish* exhalation along the ground. If she let it go, that sound would stop.

But then she would have to look behind her to pick it up.

The flashlight beam arced to the right, casting lean shadows through the trees. Alicia caught a cluster of gaunt faces as if a circle of thin naked men sat in the woods, turning to peer over their bony shoulders as the flashlight arced away. They were gone when Margaret's light returned to the right.

A chill quaked through Alicia. "When you said *Maybe this side*? You weren't talking about which side of the road, were you?"

Margaret didn't answer.

Alicia's breath rushed out. "Jesus. You're scared too, aren't you?"

Margaret remained quiet for another moment, and then whispered, "Yes."

"Christ and fuck." The words barely climbed Alicia's throat.

She squeezed her arms against her sides, desperate to keep her hands from trembling any worse, failing at every step. She almost wanted to close her eyes and keep from seeing what Margaret's flashlight found next.

Swish-swish.

Her spine shot icicle-straight at the sound. No, she must've misheard the jacket behind her, its dragging noise turning into an unending breath, sure, but not the sleeve-against-side rhythm of someone walking while wearing it. Not like the sound she'd heard in her house.

She slowed her steps into a glacial crackle across dead leaves.

Swish-swish.

Alicia craned her neck forward and stiffened the tendons. If she didn't make it hurt to try looking back, she might do it on reflex. She couldn't let that happen. Her eyes focused on Margaret's puffy coat, her sweeping flashlight.

Resistance pressed between Alicia's fingers, splitting them around the jacket. It felt full and swollen, as if a thin arm had shoved through its turquoise fabric sleeve.

"Margaret," Alicia tried to say, but her mouth had no spit and barely any volume. "Margaret? I don't think we're alone."

Margaret slowed her flashlight's arc. "We never were."

Alicia gritted her teeth. "Can you get an ounce of bedside manner? Or at least look back and see what's with me? Please?"

"No, ma'am," Margaret said, her sternness faltering. "I can't look behind you. You can't look behind you. We're in uncertain places now, and if we look back, we could make a presence certain. And if we do that, it might never leave. Is that what you want?"

Alicia didn't answer. What she wanted was her warm bed, and a smoke, but one hand was full of something—someone. She wanted to go the hell home.

Her breath rushed out in another wispy cloud, only visible where it crossed her view of Margaret's flashlight. She sucked in chilly air and held it trapped in her lungs. Let it get warm, let her breath slow.

Swish-swish.

Someone else's breathing slid behind her with the jacket sound, ruffling her hair.

Alicia slowed her steps, letting Margaret get a few yards farther ahead. Uneven steps thumped behind her, uncertain of her pace. There was someone in her grip, at her back, at her heels, and she wasn't allowed to turn and see who it was. That shadow she'd glimpsed before? One of the gaunt men come to get an up-close look at her?

She wished she really was leading Natalie by the arm. Better to be in that shattered house of grief than in these woods with this callous witch and the legion of unknowns.

Best if Alicia could see her sister and niece again and not vanish here.

Her eyes burned with fresh tears, and she lowered her eyelids against them. There would only be uncertainty now. Only the darkness, the cold, the sense of substance within her grip, and the sounds of footsteps, and breathing, and *swish-swish* behind her.

Beside her.

Tugging her to the left in a clumsy lead.

"Margaret," she snapped. "Margaret!"

She went on calling, but she kept her eyes squeezed shut, didn't want to see what was dragging her, didn't want to look by mistake.

The world slid by in a black rush of mashing leaves and swatting branches. She was part of this ghostly land now, this ghost world, a kind she'd never imagined in her mundane life, one she wanted desperately to forget. If only she'd given the jacket to the driver, everything could be as it was. Let it haunt him instead.

But she couldn't let go of the jacket now. Couldn't quit running and shouting for Margaret.

Until her boot slammed against a soft lump, forcing Alicia to yank back and let her eyes flash open.

Pale cheeks and a shining glare reared through the dark ahead.

Alicia crossed her arms in front of her face. "I'm sorry!" she shrieked, her voice hoarse. "Jesus, it was an accident!"

The world went still around her. She lowered her arms in cautious inches and peeked beneath her eyelids, vaguely aware of Margaret's tromping footsteps getting nearer and nearer.

Tears burst down Alicia's cheeks as the jacket dropped limp beside her. "I looked," she said. "I didn't mean to, it startled me—"

"Hush, hush," Margaret said, and a steadying hand found Alicia's shoulder. "We're not in uncertain places anymore."

Her flashlight eased over the ground between two white-barked trees and settled past Alicia's boots, where a figure lay amid crisscrossing roots. A holey pastel pink sweater covered the face. Black fluid stained the once-blue jeans. Darker was the crater opening the figure's middle, but it was long past exhaling any odor into the woods.

Alicia stared into the gaping hole and waited for eerie dream-eyes to peer out. She then waited to find herself hunched inside, looking up at the black sky and the cold world beyond the body that had to be the jacket's true owner.

But nothing changed. Alicia remained standing over the prone figure, turned husklike since first collapsing here in the woods. Margaret kept her flashlight aimed at the ground, but her head turned away from the corpse.

"Hang on." Alicia trembled back a step. "Was this what it was? Did you know someone was dead out here?"

"I suspected," Margaret said.

"But how'd she get here?" Alicia flailed clawing hands. "What the hell?"

"I imagine your Good Samaritan would know more." Margaret gave the body another glance, and then she turned around and began to walk. Her boots scuffed the earth, forming a discernible path in the forest floor. "Try to make a mess on the way out. It'll give the authorities an easier trail to follow from the road after you call them."

Alicia watched Margaret shrink step by step. "Turn that light this way," she said. "I dropped the jacket."

"They'll take the jacket now." Margaret coughed into her arm, less like choking, more like trying to keep from throwing up. "And the body."

Alicia stepped from the dead person, the jacket, and every leafy crunch dragged realization up her nerves. "Are you saying we're done? That's it?"

Margaret said nothing. She took another step away, and another.

"Wait, wait, that can't be it," Alicia said, hurrying to catch up. "There has to be more. We don't know what happened to her. How'd she end up here? What the hell's wrong with this place?"

"This place?" Margaret asked. "We're in the woods off Route 29. If we were ever somewhere else, we aren't there now."

Alicia gaped. "But what about the driver? The guy who did this? What do we do about him?"

"Do we know he did this? How he found the jacket? And what could you do if it was his fault?" Margaret turned and gripped Alicia's arm, a glare burning through her spectacles. "You brushed with death and got away. Leave it, Ms. Meadows."

A hole ate at Alicia's middle. "But he might have killed other people."

"Isn't that why you left your sister's house that night?" Margaret asked. "Wasn't it suffocating you? Killing you? We walk away from things that might kill us. You don't know what happened here. And knowing might be worse than not knowing. Neither of us will likely ever find out unless I can convince one of my colleagues to visit, and I'm not going to put a medium through that. They have it hard enough as it is. No, we walk away now. Understand? Leave it."

"You're telling me to try to forget all that?" Alicia asked, disbelieving.

Margaret slid her fingers down Alicia's forearm and patted the back of her hand. "I'm suggesting you live. As much as you can."

It took them less time to reach Route 29 than to find the body. Alicia briefly wondered what exact woods they had been walking through in the dark, the anywhere woods of some otherworld, but then she let the curiosity fade.

Margaret might be right. It was better not to know.

Alicia waved before sliding into her car, but she didn't look to see if Margaret waved back. Meeting that woman once was enough. She had no idea how to handle what else she might have seen in those woods.

At the gas station, she slid coins into the nearby payphone and dialed nine-one-one. She told the operator she'd found a body off Route 29 and could lead the authorities to it. They told her to wait.

And she waited, seated on the hood of her car and facing the grim night. There was enough time for her to smoke a cigarette at last, and she could make a wintertime snowfall of the ashes draping the gas station asphalt.

A realization snowed in with them—it could've been her, too. Margaret had a point, they didn't know the truth, but if Alicia's suspicion had merit, the driver might have been teasing himself with picking up dark-haired, wild-eyed Alicia, if not to hurt her, then gearing his nerves to hurt someone else.

Alicia might have been a stepping stone toward his next pick-up, his next body in the woods. Maybe he let some get away. But he kept others.

And she had no idea where he was. Only the jacket he'd lent and the person he left, and kept, and that she had gotten away. There was nothing she could do about that.

Lucky you, the driver had said, his teeth glaring white.

Smoke blew through Alicia's lips as blue-and-red lights flickered over the gas station. "Lucky me."

NO SUCH THING AS IN GOOD HANDS

April 1979

The afternoon light bent wrong around the house, and home became a wrong place.

Margaret Willow faced ahead as she parked her car at the curb. She wouldn't look at the house again until she had no choice. The light would change by then, trickle differently through the horseshoe of green pines and elm trees where her home tucked into the woods, and she could dismiss that *wrong* feeling. It wasn't real. She was no medium, absorbing sentiments from a moment or lifting information from inanimate objects with a clairvoyant fingertip. All these phenomena were possible, but not from her.

She shut off the car, climbed from the driver's seat, and lifted two brown paper bags of groceries from the back. This would be a quiet evening. The woods were still and dewy with fresh springtime, and she would make dinner tonight, and a baguette's end jutted from one bundle, the very model of a grocery bag on its way home.

The light bent again as she turned toward the house. She was no medium, fine, but she was a living creature, and she believed in the subconscious breadth of human instinct to pick up subtle clues, unnoticed by the present mind, and ram them with crackling clarity through the nervous system.

What had she noticed and yet missed as she pulled up to the curb?

A light breeze in the tree branches. The weed-thick lawn. A white Chevy in the driveway, where it belonged. Darkness in the windows between stretches of the house's baby blue siding. White flat stones forming the walkway from street to stoop.

And Trish Patel ahead of that stoop, pacing back and forth over the short width of the last walkway stone in a one-two, one-two stride. Her arms crossed her chest, and a grim line set in her thin brown face.

Why would she wait outdoors? Evening would bring a chill soon, and when Trish had a bad day—a lecture opportunity falling through, an unpleasant call or letter from her siblings back in London—she usually busied herself around the kitchen, the living room, trying again to sort the boxes in the attic, never one to sit idle.

Which meant the wrong was coming from inside the house.

Margaret clacked her shoes along the walkway stones and squeezed her bags. Their loud crinkling made Trish stop mid-pace, where her expression curdled into clenched teeth and dark, worried eyes. How long had she been pacing out here, awaiting Margaret's return?

"She wouldn't talk to me," Trish said, hurrying the words together.

"Who?" Margaret asked, reaching her.

"She wouldn't give me a name." Trish glanced toward the picture window. "But she wrote yours on her hand. She knows you."

Margaret set the grocery bags down on the walkway. The heavier one teetered, threatening to spill its baguette onto the stone. She stepped onto the lawn toward the picture window, at first only seeing her pink-faced reflection, and then beyond that opened the gloomy living room.

Blue TV light flickered down the gaunt face of Hope Magnussen. She sat hunched on the floor a foot from the television set, the tension of twenty-four years tightening her pale expression into a hateful glare.

Margaret crept back from the glass and toward the walkway. What the hell was Hope doing here? They hadn't seen each other in six months, maybe seven. She had been thicker set then, more like Margaret, but now her skin hugged her bones.

This couldn't be about that noise. Margaret had tried to help Hope deal with her unusual haunting—if that was what it had been. They hadn't come to a solid conclusion. That was the trouble, the reason Margaret let Hope go, sending her off to another expert in the supernatural. Hope was one of theirs, a true medium. In the hands of someone more experienced, there was no reason she couldn't have cut her haunting from her soul. This had nothing to do with Margaret anymore.

A soft hand slid onto her shoulder. "You told me none of this kind of work would follow you home," Trish said. "I understand when it's helping childbirth, but not this."

"That work didn't follow me," Margaret said, laying her hand over Trish's. "Hope isn't a problem. She's a colleague." At least, she used to be.

"But she *has* a problem, Maggie." Trish leaned into Margaret's side. "Something's not right."

Margaret would've liked nothing more than to turn around, bury her face in Trish's cloud of dark hair, and get on with their evening.

But this was their home. Even if Hope had made it a wrong place.

"Stay here," Margaret said.

She couldn't remember her hand ever trembling when reaching for this doorknob. Maybe from cold, but not like this. Her nerves, busy in their unconscious work, must have noticed something else through the window besides a familiar face. She worked at the image, bringing details together as she passed the kitchen and turned toward the living room entrance.

Darkness broken by flickering blue, Hope's narrowed eyes, her blond hair having lost some luster, she might not have bathed in a few days, her arms slung over her lap and between her legs, Trish saying Hope had written Margaret's name on her hand—

Had Margaret seen that hand? Yes, but not the writing. She'd seen something else, only noticing it in mind as she spotted it in the living room now.

A black pistol dangled from Hope's left hand.

She glanced up as Margaret lifted her foot, uncertain whether to retreat into the hall or take another step forward. There was no hiding her presence—Hope had the TV on but muted. She'd heard every anxious footfall.

"Hope?" Margaret swallowed hard and thought she tasted metal. She might have bitten her tongue without realizing. "We weren't expecting you."

Hope raised her right hand. Her two longest fingers gripped a black marker between them as if she were a child pretending to clutch a cigarette. Sweat-smeared ink bore a single name across her lined palm—*Margaret*. The letters were sloppy, written by a non-dominant hand.

"Yes," Margaret said. "You scared someone important to me, coming here. I need you to leave our house."

Hope raised her left hand—that gun hand—and showed the back. Beneath her knuckles stretched a brief sentence, written in anticipation. *I still hear it.*

Margaret stiffened. The haunting hadn't gone away then.

"I'm sorry for that," she said. She set her foot down on the living room carpet and leaned deeper into the gloom. "But I referred you to Professor Mbaye in Pittsburgh. Did you meet her? Talk to me."

Hope pursed her lips and shook her head. Several strands of once-blond hair had turned white since summer. Red canyons wormed from one ear to her neck, carved by fingernails. She wore a ragged T-shirt, and she'd knotted the sleeves of her old bomber jacket around her waist, same as when she used to lead séances in the homes of people who weren't really haunted but wanted to think so.

Margaret had warned her about playing with fire. A more apt analogy might have been, *Dangle raw meat in the woods long enough and something hungry might finally show up.*

Hope pincered her fingers against the TV's front and turned a dial. She'd been chewing her nails. The volume slowly climbed.

Margaret slipped deeper into the living room, enough to see the screen, as a pre-recorded commotion filled the air. Mustached men in overalls charged with shotguns over a dark knoll. Margaret recognized a TV movie she'd seen at its first broadcast years ago, *The Night That Panicked America*, retelling the events surrounding Orson Welles and his Halloween 1938 radio adaptation of *The War of the Worlds*.

This broadcast was late in the movie, when one of the militiamen ready to fight the Martians leaned toward his truck. Margaret vaguely remembered that the man should have overheard another actor portraying Orson Welles giving a late-show disclaimer.

But the audio made no sense. Instead of a stern voice telling America to calm the hell down, a warped reverberation slid through the truck. The sonic wave of a modern electric guitar echoed a finished note, ground its teeth into static, and then swerved into another aural vibration of anachronistic contempt.

The actors spoke their lines without any change, their past performances trapped in celluloid fate. Only the radio was different, overwritten in Hope's presence. Any other television tuned to this channel would play the movie right, but with Hope here, the sound came changed. Haunted, like her.

The TV's blue flicker reflected in her teary eyes. She blinked hard at Margaret as if asking a silent question before returning the volume to zero.

Margaret had no answers. Not now, not back in summer when the reverberation first came growling through Hope's car stereo. And then her television. Soon it began to play over the speaker system at the grocery store while grabbing bread and milk, the mall while shopping, even the elevator at a hotel in Iowa when Hope thought a change in location might break her from this persistent sonic disease.

She'd been certain of a haunting of some kind, but neither she nor Margaret could figure out its source or reason.

Professor Nell Mbaye might have. She'd studied sensory phenomena relating to technology and had perspectives Margaret couldn't assume. But she wasn't here, and she probably knew nothing of Hope's situation.

"Why didn't you go to Pittsburgh?" Margaret asked.

The cool living room air seemed to slough down Hope's body as she aimed her pistol at the TV. Margaret tensed for a shot, cracking glass, an explosion. Hope instead dug the marker into her outstretched arm and wrote two words along her bicep.

No hope.

"Please," Margaret scoffed. "You're twenty-four years old. What do you know about hopeless? Professor Mbaye is an expert."

So was I, Hope scrawled. Why wouldn't she speak? *Told people they're in good hands. No such thing. We're liars.*

Margaret opened her mouth to argue, but her stomach clawed at her throat. Was Hope right? In the soundscape of her haunting, with Margaret having turned up no solutions and then turned her away, maybe they were all liars, and the lie was that there could be any such thing as an expert in the supernatural.

"We should try anyway." Margaret took a soft step toward the center of the living room. "If it's hopeless, you have nothing to lose. I'll take you to Professor Mbaye. We'll go together. She can help you. I can't."

Can't? Hope wrote. *Or it's too hard?*

The gun hand twitched, freezing Margaret a few feet from Hope and the TV. Her black marker must have struck a tendon.

"There was nothing else I could do for you," Margaret said, her breath shaky. "We can't dig up the past. Not the way you wanted. There's only so much any one person can do."

Hope cast mournful eyes through the gloom, and a ghostly fist clenched at Margaret's gut. No, she wouldn't feel shame for this, she hadn't given up on Hope. An expert out of her element could do more damage than good.

Or had she not wanted to risk a mistake? She knew failure in the hot blood and shit and misery of helping deliver newborns, of trying her best and finding catastrophe anyway.

The TV's glow lit across Hope's bicep. *We're liars.*

Maybe the lie had nothing to do with the existence of experts. Maybe the real lie was Margaret's—that there were indeed such things as experts in the supernatural, but how dare she count herself among them when she would turn this young woman away?

Hope went on jotting words along her arm. *Bird at window this morning. Tried to sing. Know what came out?* She pointed to the muted television, as if she could hear the haunting noise even with the volume turned down.

"It's spread to living things?" Margaret asked.

Hope shut her eyes. *Not alive*, she wrote without looking, and then she jerked the pistol backward as if absorbing a gunshot's recoil. *No sound when died. Other birds, no song.*

Margaret shuddered and then inched along the carpet. "I don't know how to make it stop. That's why we need to find you some other help. *Real* help. It can't be me."

Hope swung her left arm and aimed the pistol at Margaret. Her right hand clawed the hem of her T-shirt up from her belly, where she scribbled clumsy letters down the side of her abdomen.

Gave up on me.

"I didn't," Margaret said, too quickly. The pistol's black eye stared through her. "Hope, I'm sorry."

Hope licked her lips and stood from the floor, keeping the pistol trained on Margaret. Was it a hair trigger? Was the safety off? Margaret couldn't tell. She could only make out the tears slithering down Hope's cheeks, blinking blue, white, yellow by the TV's flicker before Hope let her mouth fall open, where everything hung black.

Sonic warping encircled her words. "It's *okaaay*." An amplifier growl rippled down her tongue. "I *gaaave* up. On me too. We're the *saaame*."

Margaret's eyes stung. She bit inside her cheek, desperate to steer heartache into physical pain, and then maybe she could trick her nerves into believing she could be strong. Even brave.

But she wasn't. Breaking from Hope to avoid one failure had only summoned another, a self-fulfilling prophecy ready to gun her down.

"I'm sorry," Margaret said again. "I should have stuck with you in summer, through autumn, winter, all of it. We should've looked into everything you could remember. Anything you'd encountered, client by client, every contact with anything strange. Or I should've never started trying to help you. Is that it?"

Hope's body jerked forward like she was coughing. Only rough static crashed up her throat. The pistol jittered in her gun hand, fingers twitching.

Margaret breathed sharply through her nose, her heart ready to burst.

Hope's spasm eased. "It's *whaaat* I learned, what I *waaant* you to know," she said. Another electric note quaked through her words. "It's *okaaay*. We *aaall* give up, Margaret. It's human for *usss* to quit. It's okay."

Her left arm bent, jutting out from her shoulder and smudging every message into an inky alphabet slush. The pistol aimed at her head. TV light glimmered over two words, meant for a bird, glaring from Hope's skin. *Not alive.*

"We can try again!" Margaret shouted. "I'll try harder, I'll do better, we'll find out where it comes from, what's causing—"

The gunshot flashed white through the room. Hot fluid spattered Margaret's face and chest, and the ringing whine of microphone feedback sang through the air as Hope struck the carpet.

Afternoon light bent through the picture window, shaped and broken by tree limb shadows. They were cast unmoving, the outside gone windless. Margaret couldn't hear her breath, her heart. The world had stopped with Hope and the gun.

Down the hall, the front door slammed open. Footsteps and silverware clattered in the kitchen, and something heavy and wooden struck the linoleum, chased by stomping up the hallway.

Trish stormed into the living room, clutching a butcher knife overhead. Her eyes stretched wide and white until they fell on Margaret, standing and alive. Trish let the knife fall to the floor and grabbed Margaret in both arms.

Margaret swayed under Trish's embrace, pivoting them so she would be the only one seeing the body.

"You're not hurt?" Trish whispered.

Margaret shook her head, rubbing her chin on Trish's shoulder. Dark hair covered her face but not enough to hide Hope, lying on the floor. She was already decaying on a microscopic level into rough fibers, her blood becoming carpet blood, her skin becoming carpet flesh, every wet surface gleaming in the TV light. The gun, too, gleamed over the growing puddle.

That dampness reached up and stroked Margaret's neck—no, only Trish, kissing her, thanking God she was alright.

No one deserved thanks besides Hope herself. She hadn't come here to hurt Margaret or Trish. She'd known where she meant to aim the pistol from the start, even if she'd let Margaret think otherwise. Margaret had done nothing to sway her, same as she'd done nothing for her last year.

It's okay, Hope's voice echoed. Not distorted by electrical reverberation, but clear, the way Hope used to sound. Like herself.

The way she might have sounded had Margaret not gotten involved. If Margaret, already involved, had stayed at Hope's side until the bitter end, investigating every possible angle and not giving up until she could turn that haunting's volume to zero, a gift of silence in a better way than a gunshot's aftermath.

We all give up, Margaret, the echo went on.

Margaret squeezed Trish against her chest and at last shut her eyes. It felt like another kind of giving up. A denial.

It's human for us to quit, Hope's echo said. *It's okay.*

But it wasn't.

THE WHISPERS OF NATALIE GLASGOW

August 1979

The heavy wooden door strained against Natalie's fingers, wrapped around the summer-warmed iron handle. She didn't want it to slam shut, but her eleven-year-old arms were thin and bony. Some days she felt her light brown hair could be thicker than her biceps when she bound it in a ponytail.

Her pale face flushed with heat, and the door won the fight. It swung the last few inches to crash within its frame, and she shuddered as if the church were shouting at her for it.

She ducked back from the door along the concrete porch, toward the steps leading to the sidewalk. Out from beneath the awning lay the parking lot, filled with parishioners' cars, plus the one she'd arrived in.

But she couldn't leave without Aunt Alicia, who stood against the porch railing and dug through her little black purse. Broad sunglasses perched atop her brow, blending with her dark hair, and her scarlet lipstick matched her jacket, all pieces of her intent on melding together until she gained a simpler form, more like one of Natalie's drawings than her mother's sister of flesh and blood.

"I can't believe you asked him that," Alicia said, a shrug in her voice. She kept her eyes on her purse. "He's a priest. Do you know what that is?"

Natalie knew but couldn't put her definition into easy words. A priest was a little like a teacher in that he explained things, often in a boring way, and you weren't supposed to talk back to him even if he was wrong.

And a priest was a little like something else, too, but that was the hard part. Something of a man, something of the church, like its ceiling had dripped stone down the inner walls and puddled until it formed a statue, and then God or an angel had brought that statue to life in the form of a white-collared man in black.

He was pretty, in a way. Natalie knew better than to tell a man that, no matter how she felt. But she hadn't known other things she shouldn't say or ask.

Alicia at last plucked a cigarette from its purse-held pack and struck a match. The tiny flame blazed at the cigarette's end, and smoke snaked toward the porch awning.

"Mom says you shouldn't do that," Natalie said.

"She says *you* shouldn't do that," Alicia said. "She's just jealous because she gave them up. I'm different. They fill me up with good feelings." She took a deep breath and let a gray wave of smoke ripple between her lips. "How about you? Did it fill you with good feelings?"

Natalie wrinkled her nose. "Smoke?"

"No, you ditz. Church."

"I don't know." Natalie glanced at the wooden door set in the white stone, taunting her in its heaviness. "How about you?"

"I don't come here," Alicia said, and she gestured at her red outfit. "Am I dressed like I come here? Besides, it's not about me. You're the glum bum. Thought we'd give this a try. I hear church is supposed to fill you up with—I don't know." She cupped her free hand, hefting an unseen bag of forgotten words. "Like, faith? Meaning? Something to tell you, hey, all the shit you're going through? There's a mysterious reason."

Natalie blinked at her.

Alicia dropped her curled hand and brought the other to her lips. "No? God's a bust?"

There was no good answer, but Natalie was pretty sure you weren't supposed to say things like that about God on the church's porch. Maybe Aunt Alicia could get away with it outside the priest's earshot. Or because she was grown. Natalie should've asked someone else to ask the priest her question.

"Fine, no good feelings here," Alicia said, and she let her sunglasses drop over her eyes. "How about ice cream?"

A calm breeze slid over the small tree-encircled park, where a wood-paneled ice cream stand mounted two open windows over its broad countertop. Above jutted a wooden plaque painted up like a giant banana sundae.

Both Natalie and Alicia stuck to simple ice cream cones. They wrapped the lattice wafers in napkins and carried them to the rows of picnic tables lining the blacktop between the ice cream stand and the parking lot. A green lawn spread to one side, its edges shaded by trees, its center home to a roughshod gravel playground full of little kids.

Their screams and squeals jumped through a rumbling summer insect chorus, audible yet unseen. The usual flies that buzzed around garbage cans and picnic tables were absent, maybe hiding from the merciless sun.

Natalie sat on a bench attached to one picnic table and set her shoulders against the table's edge, facing the green. Alicia sat on the tabletop and planted her sneakers beside Natalie. A cigarette smoldered in one hand while the other gripped a chocolate cone.

"I should've brought sunblock," Alicia said, adjusting her sunglasses. "Your arms are getting red already. Try to stay under the slide or the trees if you go playing with those kids when you're done."

Natalie licked her vanilla scoop. "I'm too old."

"Christ, baby girl, pop me in a sarcophagus then." Alicia blew smoke, licked her ice cream, and took another drag. "So, your mom find another job yet?"

Natalie's mother never told her anything about that, said it wasn't a little girl's problem to worry about layoffs and interviews. Like she was five and not eleven—twelve in two months.

"Is she changing her name back?" Alicia asked. "That might help. Meadows is a good name. It always suited her better than me. Heather Meadows. Alicia Meadows. She had that double *eh* locked down."

For Natalie's entire life, she'd shared the same last name as both her parents. What would it mean, with her father gone, if her mother changed from Glasgow? Would Natalie have to change her last name too, or would a division line carve between them?

"Ask her," Natalie said.

Alicia scoffed an orb of smoke. "She doesn't talk to me. She talks to you."

Natalie was quiet for a moment. "She doesn't talk to anyone."

"Isn't that just like her?"

Alicia dug into her ice cream scoop, all lips and teeth, as if she'd said something wrong and couldn't cram chocolate into her mouth fast enough. Melted ice cream burbled over the side of the cone. The scoop rolled past Alicia's fingers, struck her jeans, and fell between the table and the bench where it plopped onto the shadowed asphalt.

"Son of a bitch—you didn't hear that." Alicia tilted her cone like gravity could grow it a new head, and then she turned to Natalie. "Hey, let me lick yours."

"What?" Natalie peeped. "But it's mine."

"Oh come on." Alicia craned over Natalie's head.

Natalie hunched over her cone and stuck out a protective arm. "No, it's mine!" she cried, laughing.

"One lick for Aunt Alicia!"

"You'll make it taste bad!"

"Taste bad?" Alicia stood off the table and stepped onto the blacktop. "I warned Heather you'd turn into a snob around here. Fine, I'll get my own. Maybe a sundae. It'll be bigger and better. Who the hell likes vanilla anyway?"

She strode past, giving Natalie a playful shove along the way. Natalie giggled and watched Alicia step to the end of the growing line at the ice cream stand.

The sun had a temper today, each harsh ray battering the picnic tables and cars. Natalie had to lap at the sides of her cone to keep it from drooling vanilla over her fingers.

A child's shriek turned her eyes to the green lawn and its playground. The kids were avoiding the monkey bars, their hot iron flaking red paint. A steel spinner gleamed over a gravel bed, ready to melt all the ice cream in the world. Even the slide couldn't be safe. Its ladder was splintery wood, and its descent jutted with sharp sides and stuck out a glaring metal tongue.

Every surface shined with pain. When had Natalie started caring about that? She couldn't remember. Hot surfaces and skinned knees and palms never bothered her when she was little. Playground caution had always seemed like a grown-up concern. Was she grown now? No one treated her like she was, and adults knew better than to ask inappropriate questions of priests, but this restlessness in her chest—she could ease it by running manic on that playground, and yet having fun sounded like too much work.

If only the church had filled her with good feelings like Alicia had hoped. Natalie might have seen a point to running around then. Sitting with ice cream was easier.

Her eyes readjusted to looking at her cone the moment a white shape fluttered onto the stunted vanilla mound. Natalie stretched her arm, tearing the cone away from her face.

A moth had landed on her ice cream. It didn't float away at her sudden movement, and it didn't look stuck in the vanilla swamp. Maybe refreshed by the cold, it pattered in circles, more like a fly than a moth.

Natalie wasn't sure what to do if it didn't want to leave. She tried to imagine she wasn't here with Alicia, that instead her father sat on the bench beside her, his arms parked on the picnic table, facing the opposite way, like he was keeping watch in one direction while Natalie guarded the other.

If he saw the moth on her ice cream, he would lean over and tell her what to do. He'd been harsh sometimes, and he might've told her to wave the insect away and either eat her ice cream or toss it.

But he used to be encouraging, too. He might've convinced Natalie that the tough thing to do, the grown-up thing, was to lick the moth-touched ice cream. Reclaim it.

Except he wasn't going to be any sort of way toward her anymore. The church couldn't bring him back. It certainly hadn't drained the unease from Natalie's body or thoughts. Hell, it couldn't even give Alicia whatever word she'd been searching for on its porch, powerless as ice cream to mend these uncomfortable feelings.

"Can you?" Natalie asked, narrowing her eyes at the moth. "If I was like you, I wouldn't know anything, would I? Moths don't miss Daddy."

The moth pattered another circle around the liquifying ice cream. Its wings waved up and down, pretending it might take off. Natalie sat mesmerized by their white trembling.

A raspy whisper slinked in beside her. "Are you going to eat him?"

Natalie snapped her head to the right. There was a flash of her father, that imagined presence, but no—another man sat on the bench.

His face was gray and grim, aimed at Natalie. Red veins shot through his eyes, the way Natalie's looked on nights she'd stayed up too late. The sun gleamed down his damp bald head. He hunched toward the playground, wearing a black suit and white button-up. Maybe he'd come from a funeral or was heading to one later. His jacket flapped at his chest with the breeze, fabric wafting around jutting bones, and white moths fluttered underneath. His white shirt might have been full of them.

"Did you hear me, little girl?" he asked. "I said, are you going to eat him? He got away from me, but he came to you. I don't want to be rude."

"What?" Natalie asked, jaw trembling.

The moth-jacket man tilted his head. "I'll take that as a no."

His mouth yawned open, and he thrust it onto the cone. Natalie held stone-stiff, forgetting how to move, could only watch as a lumpy purple tongue stroked the top of her cone, its vanilla hill. It caught the moth on a muscly tip and curled chalky wings into the man's mouth.

A joyful hum seeped through his lips. His eyelids lowered, pleased, ready for sleep.

The purple tongue snaked out again, lapped at the cone, slid back, out again, giving up on moths and craving only vanilla sludge.

Its tip stroked one of Natalie's clutching fingers.

Her fist squeezed in reflex, crunching the napkin-swaddled cone, and then flinched open, dropping the whole mess onto the asphalt.

The moth-jacket man's hum lowered to a groan. "Now, you shouldn't have done that," he whispered. "Waste of a good bug lure. Haven't you heard? You catch more with sweet things than vinegar."

He licked his lips, moths rising from under his collar, over his scalp, and then he widened his bloodshot eyes. His body hunched all the way forward, tipping him off the bench.

He then dodged back along the picnic table as Alicia bore down on him, her sneaker stamping over Natalie's fallen ice cream, her sunglasses shaken from one eye, a cigarette aiming knifelike from her pincered fingers.

"Get the fuck away from her or I'll burn your eyes out!"

Kids slowed on the green and gravel, a few of their small faces turning to the blacktop at the echoing curse. Families glanced from neighboring picnic tables, and the general insect chorus quieted, the part Natalie hadn't realized came from human conversation.

The moth-jacket man scrambled back until his hip struck another picnic table. He then twisted around and dashed toward the parking lot, where he disappeared amid the gleaming cars. The air in his wake was clear of moths.

Alicia dropped her cigarette and folded a protective arm around Natalie. They held still, watching the half-smoked cigarette burn on the asphalt beside the growing vanilla puddle until the usual commotion returned to the picnic tables and park, rejoining the insect drone in the trees.

"It's okay," Alicia said, tamping down her voice. "You're good, we're good. All's good. He won't be coming back."

Natalie scraped her shoe at the ground. Drops of white ice cream had splattered the side. Alicia grabbed a napkin from her purse and wiped a vanilla smear off the ankle of Natalie's jeans.

"I'll get you a new cone," Alicia said.

But Natalie shook her head. "I want to go home."

Alicia's rickety car quaked with impatience at the lip of the Glasgow driveway. Natalie wouldn't make it wait long. She popped out of the passenger's side, waved goodbye, and started away.

"Hey, baby girl." Alicia had reached across the passenger's seat and rolled down the window. "Your mom should be home soon?"

It sounded like a question, but Natalie wasn't sure about that, or the right answer. She nodded anyway.

"Do me a favor—don't tell her," Alicia said. "About the park."

"Why?" Natalie asked.

"She's skittish. It's you and her in that house, that's all. We have to take care of her, and this'll scare her." Alicia raised her sunglasses. "You don't want to scare her, do you?"

Natalie pursed her lips.

Alicia patted the car door. "Come on, Nat, throw me a bone here. I'll keep your secrets, you keep mine."

Had Natalie done anything that needed to be kept a secret? Maybe without realizing it, and Alicia was too much the fun aunt to point it out, only smirking outside Natalie's sight without needing to scold or correct.

"Okay," Natalie whispered.

"You're a trooper," Alicia said. She tapped her palm to her lips and blew a loud kiss. "Mwah! Don't behave too much!"

She then rolled up the window and roared from the driveway, her car glittering with August sunshine.

The house was quiet inside, its air stagnant. Natalie shut the door and reached for the living room wall switch, but then she let her hand fall away. She couldn't have explained why, had anyone stood here to ask. The light would have been an intruder, and she needed a moment alone with her unquiet thoughts.

Her fingers were sticky with ice cream. And hopefully nothing else. She should wash them.

She instead marched deeper into the living room and slammed a couch pillow over her head. A raspy whisper had her by the ear, and she needed it to let go, to be dissuaded by the pillow and leave, just goddamn leave.

"Please," she said.

In the wake of her request, another sound reached for her. It was softer than the moth-jacket man's whisper, like fingertips lightly stroking wooden slats.

She dropped the pillow and turned to the short hall reaching from the living room's back, where stood the wood-slatted double doors of her father's study.

"Daddy?"

The sound came again, fluttering, an echo of windswept clothes on a backyard laundry line. Natalie circled the couch and followed, the noise growing louder as she approached the double doors. Her mother usually kept them locked, the way her father had when he was alive. Natalie liked to try them sometimes anyway, just in case.

One door folded open. The inner study was black, its windows and back door curtained, its lights off. With the living room left dark, there was little to breach the gloominess within.

"Daddy?" Natalie called again.

White wings flashed into her eyes, her face. She blustered backward, sputtering and smacking frantic hands through the air.

A cloud of moths folded around her head and danced into the living room.

Natalie held still for a long moment, listening for a raspy whisper and daring the study's darkness to cough up the moth-jacket man. A sticky sensation on her skin warned that she might've torn off a sliver of his presence and taken him home.

The study slowly deepened, forming uncertain shapes. There was no man inside. Natalie let out a breath and turned around.

White wings dripped from the air in a rainfall of dying insects. They must have been poisoned together or had starved in unison. Maybe they were never meant to live in the first place.

Natalie trembled. She was supposed to do something, wasn't she? Clean away the bodies. Vacuum them up, or wait for her mother to do it.

She lowered herself to the carpet, first on all fours, and then on her belly, and crawled until her eye leaned close to the fallen moths. The white of their wings matched the priest's collar. Natalie thought of asking them the question she'd asked him. There was no rule against asking moths a question, and her curiosity about which things had souls and which didn't sort of concerned them. They were things, too.

Instead she pressed her tongue against her pursed lips, and then between her lips, and stuck its tip toward the fallen moths. She couldn't see it clearly, only a fuzzy red shape beneath her cheeks and nose, but it hadn't turned purple. Nothing like the moth-jacket man's tongue, reaching for that first pattering moth.

These moths didn't patter across a vanilla landscape. They lay unmoving on the carpet. There was no desire or struggle in them, only a welcome stillness. A peace in death.

That was it, the word Aunt Alicia had been grasping for on the church porch earlier today—*peace*. She'd meant for the church give peace to Natalie.

"It was never there," Natalie whispered to the dead moths, her bottom lip grazing the carpet fibers. "You knew that, huh? They didn't want me to think about death. Like I'm a little kid. Go play tag in the park. Skin your knee. Eat your ice cream."

She forced herself to stop blinking and kept her eyes trained on the moths, on death. If she did this right, she could sink into their deathful peace. She could learn from these little white shapes.

And maybe from other deaths.

That sound brushed her ears again, clearer now that one of the study doors hung open. It was nothing like moth-jacket man's pleased hum, the flapping fabric around his ribcage. This was a softer rumble, the speech of soft earth, and Natalie could imagine running her hands along its surface.

Gentle as a quiet death in the dark of her father's study.

THE POSSESSION OF NATALIE GLASGOW

September, 1979

1 The Eyes

A match flared across a white matchbook and lit the end of Heather Glasgow's cigarette. She had managed to quit before Natalie was conceived. Nathaniel drew a line in the sand on that, said he wouldn't put a child in her until "you quit treating your mouth like a goddamn ashtray." Never mind that he smoked his pipe abroad with his friends.

Never mind, because he'd been dead ten months now, because over a decade was a long time between cigarettes, and because after these past two weeks, Heather was entitled to a smoke. She cracked the window of her second-floor bedroom and let the cigarette's smoldering end stare into the dusky evening.

"It should be happening by now, shouldn't it?" Margaret Willow asked.

She sat on the end of Heather's king size bed and faced the door, her hands clasped around some gizmo with a microphone taped to the end. She was a stocky woman in her mid-forties, dressed in a black blazer, button-up shirt, and slacks. When she turned to look at Heather, the orange glow of dusk reflected in her slim spectacles.

Supposedly she was a midwife. Heather's sister said she was a witch.

"It's around now," Heather said. She sounded calmer than usual. Witch or midwife, Margaret's presence was reassuring. No one else had stayed in the house overnight these past two weeks. Besides Natalie, of course. Heather didn't think that counted anymore.

Margaret peered close to her gizmo. "I'm not picking up any sound."

"You can't set your watch to her, Ms. Willow, but it'll happen."

"Do you believe there's anything I can do?"

Heather blew smoke through the open window. "I don't, really."

"Do you believe there's anything the doctors can do?"

"She has another test tomorrow. Deep down, I think I've exhausted their capabilities." There was no other reason for Heather to call a woman like Margaret. She glanced down the length of the cigarette. "Will this upset your machines?"

"No, ma'am."

"Then do you want one?"

"It's not my poison of choice, but thank you." Margaret lifted her device and stretched it toward the door.

Heather wondered if she'd feel so relaxed when it actually started. Probably not. Best to take one more drag before she lost her nerve and the cigarette fell out of her trembling hands.

"It feels like when Nate would come home after a week or so away. Some of the time, I mean. Sometimes he'd come home and we'd be over the moon to see him. But some nights, he'd come home from his trips drunk. Went a few rounds with some of his friends on the way home, or with absolute strangers at the airport. I'd wake up hearing him stomp around out there, wait for him to come in and find out if he was angry with me."

Elsewhere in the house, another bed's springs groaned.

Margaret perked up.

Heather dropped her cigarette, as predicted. She picked it up again and snuffed it out in the ashtray. Her hands could scarcely hold onto it even then. Tonight, like every night since the first night, she was sure she would have to wriggle out this window and bust her leg in a jump to the lawn.

At least tonight she wasn't alone. At the very least if Margaret was a weirdo, she was more likely to believe that one of Natalie's nocturnal episodes was a terrifying ordeal.

Natalie's bedroom door creaked open.

"Here's our star." Margaret tilted the device in her hands. "Strong signal."

Heather licked her lips. She could still taste the fallen cigarette. "Could you please not speak?" she asked.

Margaret didn't acknowledge her, just kept her eyes on her device. A black cord ran from the microphone's box to a set of machines where black tape spooled between wheels. Watching Margaret's nervous hands fumble with her machine almost made Heather feel brave.

Natalie's door finished its awful opening cry, and then for the next minute or so there was nothing.

Heather knew the next part was coming. It was like this every night, but she dreaded it all the same.

The hallway floor groaned underfoot. Then again, as Natalie took another step.

Margaret sat up even straighter. Her right eye twitched at every creak in the floor outside, every note that said the wooden boards were sagging under a pensive force. "How much—" She swallowed and forced herself to turn back over her shoulder. "How much does she weigh?"

"She's eleven years old," Heather said. She didn't need to give a specific weight. Whatever set foot out there and made those heavy steps had to be far stronger and heavier than any eleven-year-old girl in the world.

And each step brought it closer. It was the patient pace of a predator, every movement calculated.

The next footfall landed in front of Heather's bedroom door. The floorboards bent enough that the gap between floor and door widened. Whatever prowled outside pressed itself against the door and set the wood leaning tight against its steel hinges.

Margaret inched backward, deeper into the bed.

"Don't move," Heather whispered. "Don't make a sound."

Margaret clenched her teeth and then pursed her lips. Her hands had gone white, latched around that device. Surely the microphone had captured every groan Natalie pressed into the wood. If it was even Natalie.

The presence held against the door. Then it took another step and the door relaxed, as if it had tensed up in apprehension the same as Margaret and Heather. The creak in the floorboards made a stiff line down the hall.

Heather's heart found its proper rhythm when she heard the first stairway step groan. Natalie was headed downstairs.

Margaret scooted to the edge of the bed. She pulled a handkerchief from the pocket of her blazer and dabbed at her forehead. "I wish I didn't sweat so damn much."

Heather reached for another cigarette. "Was it everything you'd hoped for?"

"I don't hope for this." Margaret shoved her handkerchief back inside her pocket. She was still sweating. "Always, it's better if I'm not needed."

"And are you needed?"

Margaret looked into Heather's eyes. There was no reflection of sunset in those spectacles now, only the clear glass that separated Heather from Margaret's stare. "I think so."

"You're awfully perturbed. I thought it would only be me."

"I'm an expert on this kind of thing, Mrs. Glasgow. I'll tell you something no other expert would. You're never desensitized to the strange. It's always fresh. And when it's scary once, it'll be scary again." Margaret turned to the door. "Have you ever gone out there?"

Heather thought for a moment. "The first night it happened, I didn't realize it was her. I went out while she was downstairs, thinking it was someone in the house, and went to her room. It was empty, of course. Hurried myself to the stairs, but that's when I saw her. She didn't notice me, but I saw the eyes." She realized she hadn't lit her new cigarette yet. "Imagine that. A mother running from her little girl."

"You did the smart thing. I wish I could do the same." Margaret approached the door and yanked it open.

Heather started up. "You can't!"

"I have to confirm what we're dealing with. Not because I want to. You have to understand that." Margaret's hands wouldn't stop shaking. "It's absolutely not because I want to." And then she left the room, into the hall.

Heather didn't follow. She couldn't even manage to get out of her chair to shut the door.

***

Margaret would've liked nothing more than to retreat from the hall and lock the bedroom door until morning when, according to Heather, this episode would end.

But how would that help Natalie?

The floor looked worn, but Natalie's path hadn't caused any permanent damage. The stairway to the first floor appeared likewise unharmed. Down below, there came a familiar, sticky click, the opening of a refrigerator door.

Margaret took to the stairs one soft step at a time. Natalie would be distracted by her strange nocturnal diet. Margaret wouldn't get a better chance to perform the church's tests. The Catholic Church was a tedious and overly bureaucratic organization when it came to this kind of problem, but in many regards they were right to be. You couldn't assume what was wrong. There had to be evidence.

The heat hit Margaret as she reached the last couple of steps. There was a dry atmosphere on the first floor of the Glasgow house that hadn't been there when she arrived in the late afternoon to meet Heather in the safety of autumn daylight. This was a blazing summer afternoon. If she spotted steam rise out of Natalie's mouth and nose, she supposed that would be a sign.

Only the ceiling lamp from the upstairs hallway cast any light through the first floor across the living room carpet into the tiled kitchen, but what little Margaret saw made her sweat even worse.

Natalie stood in the kitchen's gloom. She wore a white nightgown. Her hair frizzed at the ends, each strand suffering in the heat. Her skin was flushed and a damp sheen coated her face.

She was rummaging in the fridge, attracted to the bait her mother left for her. Heather said the episodes could go on for five or six hours, but leaving food out seemed to cut the time in half.

Not just any food. Meat, the rarer the better. Heather said it was how her husband used to eat and Natalie had picked up the habit. Only now it was worse, because a few degrees beyond raw seemed too much for her. One morning, Heather found a frozen roast on the floor, still a block of meat-flavored ice, but Natalie had gnawed on its edges anyway.

Margaret could stomach all of that, even the unpleasant sight of Natalie's mouth chewing at shredded red hamburger meat, its gristle painted across her cheeks and chin.

It was the eyes. When Natalie faced the glow of the fridge they looked normal enough, but if she turned her head even slightly, they were eyes in the dark. Eyes in the dark that reflected the light of the upstairs. Margaret was no biologist, but she knew human eyes didn't do that.

According to the Catholic Church, the skin of one possessed by a demon would burn at the touch of water blessed by an ordained priest. Margaret drew a small, clear vial from her shirt pocket and unscrewed the cap. It would only be a few drops, hardly enough for Natalie to notice she'd been touched.

Unless it burned her, of course. She would notice then. How strong did she have to be to press the floor like that?

Margaret didn't let herself think about it. She swung the vial and droplets sailed toward the kitchen. She tensed her legs to retreat.

Nothing. Natalie grasped another fistful of raw meat and shoved it between her teeth. No burning, but no anger.

Margaret lifted a golden crucifix. All the tests had to be performed, no matter how silly. Or scary. If there was a demon inside Natalie, perhaps it wouldn't care for this symbol. Margaret didn't care for the test, either. She couldn't chuck the crucifix. She had to step into the kitchen and press it to Natalie's skin.

The heat grew worse the closer Margaret came to the fridge. If only that hellish dryness in the air were enough proof, but it wasn't. She readied to bolt. A moment's touch would tell her everything. Just had to be sure she didn't drop the damn thing.

She paused a foot away from Natalie. Drops of sweat raced along her face, around her cheeks, and down her neck. Her fingers were slick, but she kept a stern grip. Now was the time. She pressed the crucifix against Natalie's arm.

Natalie's head turned. Glowing eyes stared up at Margaret's face and a mouthful of meat glistened in the yellow fridge light.

The crucifix didn't affect Natalie, but Margaret didn't notice at first because of the sound. It was almost worse than the creaking, too-heavy footsteps upstairs. No, it was worse, she decided. Much worse.

A clicking, guttural groan slid through Natalie's throat and chest. It made her whole body tense and quake, like a muscle flexing itself into overexertion. The tremor spread through the kitchen and shook the food inside the fridge, the glasses in the cupboards, the pots and pans, the windows. It shook the crucifix out of Margaret's hands and the bones up her arm, through the rest of her body. She understood the sound and backed away from the little girl.

Natalie growled and the kitchen growled with her.

Margaret almost cried out when something touched her from behind. Just the stairway's banister. She grasped it tight. She hadn't even noticed her retreat from the kitchen.

Natalie glanced at the crucifix on the floor tile, and then returned her attention to the hamburger meat.

Church doctrine expected that the demonically possessed might speak in foreign tongues such as Aramaic or older. Margaret couldn't call that growl a proper language, but she felt if a priest was here with her, he would've counted it as a bad sign.

But the holy water and the crucifix had failed. There would be no help from the church.

Margaret turned to the stairs and started a slow climb. She supposed there was good and bad news so far in this case. Demonic possession could be ruled out. Now that only left every other possibility.

The first step creaked beneath her.

Margaret didn't turn her head. If she turned her head, she would've seen too clearly, and then she would've run, and then—she didn't want to know what would've happened then. Instead, she glanced out the corner of her eye toward the kitchen, her face unmoved from its attention on the stairway.

Natalie had left the fridge. The door hung ajar, its light showing only the abandoned plastic package and the hamburger meat that now leaked red fluid across the kitchen tiles. She had crossed the space between the kitchen, across the carpet and stone floor underneath, up to the bottom of the stairs without a sound, and only her first footfall on that creaky bottom step had given her away.

She was two steps behind Margaret.

A stillness took over. Margaret thought of a deer in headlights, but that analogy felt off. She was a deer in the woods, separated from her herd, while a creature fierce and terrible loomed over her.

Natalie was just a child. Eleven years old. Margaret guessed she outweighed her four times.

But there was something in her that growled at such a pitch that it made the kitchen tremble, that stepped so hard it made the house cry for mercy. Margaret knew there was only a small, rail-thin child behind her, but she likewise knew she wasn't as strong as a house. What lived inside Natalie could buckle her. It could break her.

Her eye fixed on that refrigerator, on the raw hamburger it illuminated.

Her hand slid up the banister, grasped firm, and she ascended two steps at once this time. Her leg carried her up. She reached for the step after the next. A little farther along the banister. It took every ounce of self-control not to charge up those steps as fast as she could, as if some primal animal fear lived inside her, perhaps all humans, a scrap of prey's panic from days long past.

The steps below creaked again. Natalie was patient. What was inside her, it knew it had given itself away with that first step. It had ears, after all. Natalie's ears.

The top of the steps wasn't too far away. Running on the stairs was death. Margaret just had to keep that in mind. If she ran, Natalie wouldn't follow with cautious, predatory steps. She would chase.

Margaret's foot hit the top of the steps. Her hand left the banister in one slippery motion and reached for the corner wall. She felt the stillness coming again, an uncertainty of what to do now that she was past the steps, and a certainty that to freeze here would be a mistake. She dragged her back foot off the previous step, toward the top. Natalie was four steps below. She would have to ascend. Margaret had a straight shot to Heather's bedroom, where the door still hung wide open.

She heard another creak. Natalie wasn't going to wait for a decision.

Margaret took another step, and as she did, slipped her arms out of her blazer. Another step and she thrust it behind her without looking. Then she ran. She had to hope the flying blazer would distract Natalie, or that whatever hid inside Natalie's skin hadn't expected Margaret to run.

She didn't hear anything at first. Then the steps creaked, a low rumble filled the space between the floors of the Glasgow house, and the steps groaned, the floorboards groaned, Natalie was on the second floor, chasing. Right behind her. About to grab her. Faster.

Heather's hand stuck out from her doorway and yanked Margaret inside. The door slammed shut. Heather and Margaret shoved against it, and it swelled against them. The presence outside insisted they let it in. Its growl rattled the doorknob, the hallway air. It didn't try to break the door down. Maybe it only understood Natalie's bedroom doorknob, not others. Maybe that was how Heather had kept it inside the house these past many nights.

The swelling eased a little, and then all the way. Heavy footfalls crossed the hall at the same deliberate pace as when Natalie first opened her bedroom door tonight. They stalked up the hallway, past Natalie's bedroom, toward the upstairs bathroom.

Heather and Margaret didn't move from the door in case their steps might give them away. Margaret could hardly see the door itself. Her spectacles had fogged a little near Natalie and been tussled when running. They needed cleaning. Margaret wished she could clean away the vision of Natalie's reflective eyes and the abandoned hamburger meat. How close she had been to those things.

Natalie neared the door again. The floor cried, but she let the door be this time. She passed them, down the hall, back down the stairs again. Soon she would be on the floor, her hands quick to stuff raw meat in her mouth.

Heather eased away from the door, back to her chair by the window. An unlit cigarette awaited her in the crook of the ashtray.

Margaret knelt beside the bed and laid her head against the comforter. Her breathing rocked her chest up and down. "I have news, at least."

"Good news?" Heather asked, hand on her heart. "Or just news?"

"Your daughter isn't possessed by a demon."

Heather paused. "Then she's crazy?"

"No, ma'am."

"Well, does she have a brain lesion? A disease? What is it? What's wrong with her?"

"Please keep your voice down," Margaret said. She could see relief in Heather's face, not because of any diagnosis. It had to be comforting to know someone else was just as afraid as she'd been these last couple weeks. "The Catholic Church's tests ruled out a demon. There's still something inside her."

"But you don't know what?"

"I may need to run different tests." Margaret's hands trembled. Even the idea of getting near Natalie again in this state sounded insane.

Heather at last lit her cigarette. "Now you sound like a doctor."

"Let me have a chance to think, Mrs. Glasgow. This isn't the medical field. They wouldn't have been able to help her."

"Why not? Because you can? You say something's inside her, but you don't know what it is. It could be a growth they couldn't detect before or a sickness—" Heather stuck the cigarette between her lips and inhaled deep. There was something she wanted to say, a crazy idea of her own, that she was too ashamed to utter aloud. Or too afraid.

Sometime past midnight, Natalie shambled back to her room. She didn't shut the door, but Margaret heard the bedsprings. She opened Heather's door only briefly to see if the coast was clear. Unrelenting heat breathed from Natalie's bedroom and filled the hall with that oppressive summer day air. Margaret crept through to close Natalie's door. Even the doorknob was warm.

"I'll be back tomorrow afternoon, after your bring Natalie home from her doctor," Margaret said. "We'll go over the recordings once I've had some sleep."

"You're going to drive this late?" Heather asked. "After what you've been through?"

"I'll sleep better not being in this house." Margaret adjusted her spectacles. "I didn't mean that to sound rude. I never do. Just, keep your door locked in case she gets up again. I'll try to learn what I can. You do the same, in your own way."

"In my own way," Heather echoed, like Margaret had a funny way of saying she disagreed.

2 Doctors

It took Heather over half a dozen handshakes before Dr. Liam Horne had introduced to her every brilliant man he'd gathered to himself today in his research facility at the Stamford campus. Heather couldn't remember any of their names.

Liam then addressed the room. "If everyone would approach the glass, we're about to begin."

The brilliant men approached the glass, some dressed in black or gray suits, some dressed in white lab coats, most of them in spectacles that made Heather think of Margaret. She had looked to have a keener eye than anyone present, but looks could be deceiving. These men were renowned in their fields, and Margaret? What exactly was Margaret's field of expertise?

"I appreciate your patience, Mrs. Glasgow," Liam said. "By now, I think a woman of less fortitude, without her husband at her side, might've done something drastic."

"Drastic?" Heather asked, as if to say, *Little old me? Drastic? Never!*

"You know, consulted a fortune teller, maybe the church, or worse, one of those smoke and juju healers. Forget I said anything. Not the kind of idea I'd expect would cross a sophisticated mind like yours, what with your husband being who he was. Damn, I miss that man."

Heather should've said something encouraging, that Nathaniel spoke fondly of Liam Horne, that he always meant to invite him on another hunting trip. Those would've been nice things to say. They weren't true. Nathaniel hardly gave Liam a second thought beyond that he was the family physician, but they were nice things. Heather didn't have space in her mind for nice things. She only had space for Natalie.

So Heather said nothing and watched her daughter through the glass.

Natalie lay strapped to a white table, her head stuck in a white cylinder. Supposedly the room was too radioactive to step inside, yet not so radioactive that she was in any danger. Heather didn't understand that, but she wasn't about to ask.

"It's mapping," Liam said. An eerie glow crossed the room beyond the glass.

"How much did you sedate her?" one of the doctors asked.

"We didn't. Part of her condition is sleep to a near-sedated extent."

"And there's nothing physically wrong?"

"We'll learn soon enough."

Heather found herself wringing her hands and lowered them to her sides, where they began to wring her dress. She had never hoped for a machine to find something wrong with her little girl before today. But today came after two hellish weeks of useless Dr. Horne, of befuddled specialists, of tests that all came back saying Natalie was perfectly fine. A basic mercury thermometer couldn't even tell Natalie's temperature was up. It was enough to make Heather scream bloody murder each time she returned to her car, while Natalie dozed away in the passenger seat.

Only Margaret seemed to understand.

It took an hour to have the results of the scan, a layout of Natalie's brain. Who she was and what she thought, every piece of her mapped out on those scans. Liam and his brilliant men groomed the results with their eyes, their spectacles, and their magnifying glasses, the little ones that too many doctors seemed to carry in their pockets where men used to keep their pocket watches. They muttered to each other, a dull rumble of speculation.

"Well?" Heather asked. "What's wrong with her?"

The murmur quieted in an instant. The men glanced at each other, glanced at Liam, as if to ask why he'd brought them here when he already had all the answers.

"Please understand, Mrs. Glasgow." Liam held up his hands in a placating gesture. "These scans—the brain is the most complex organ in the human body, perhaps the most complex organ in all biology. It can take time to go over in detail and find exactly what's causing the problem."

"But you must have a hint." The back of Heather's neck burned. She wondered if a thermometer could detect *that*. "There must be something that doesn't look right. Right? I could understand if it was just one little thing wrong with her, or even one big thing, but all these problems, all of it together, her brain should be the Rockefeller Center Christmas Tree of problems, and you can't find even one—"

Heather stopped all at once. She stared at a room of ghastly faces, growing older and more obsolete by the moment. These were brilliant men? These men thought they could help her daughter? She couldn't see it. All she saw was a look of shamed confusion that scurried in their eyes, every one of them. They were pitiable, almost children. Yes, that's it. School children who didn't know the teacher's answer, each of them taking center stage in class only to be ridiculed, and then cry for their mothers.

She looked on them with motherly eyes and spoke in a motherly, doting tone. "You don't know anything, do you? None of you do. None of you know anything at all."

3 The Study

Margaret chuckled to herself. "And the horse he rode in on?" she asked. She had just returned to the Glasgow house and heard an earful.

Heather covered her mouth and coughed out a laugh. "They didn't want to help her. The doctor brought them to show off his unique find." She kept her mouth covered through a yawn. "You'd think I would sleep through the day, being up these nights. I'll get in an hour here or there, but it's, you know." She let her voice trail off.

"But you have nightmares?" Margaret pulled a checkered notebook from her bag and sat in a tall chair, cushioned with red leather. It was Nathaniel's favorite chair, with the tall back to cradle the ghastly height of him. "I had one, too."

Heather seated herself on the sofa across the coffee table. "What was it?"

"I'm not sure." Margaret adjusted her spectacles and crossed her legs. She came off as much more confident in the daylight, without having to toy with her machine or escape an eleven-year-old. "Usually my dreams are visual. I'll remember images of them, like my brain takes a vacation through them and keeps a photo album. This was different. It was all feelings. I remember it was hot and I was afraid." Her eyes were wet behind her spectacles. "And angry. The kind of angry that makes you upset, like you'd never wish to have something worth being so angry about."

Heather couldn't have put her nightmares into those words, but Margaret described them almost exactly. "I have seen things, at least the past three nights. I can't tell what. There's a tree, but not like the pines we have outside. It's a strange tree. And there's meat on the ground. A shadow."

"You've been exposed longer." Margaret's pen danced along her notebook. "If we wait even a few more days, we might get a clearer picture."

"We can't wait." Heather's nails scraped at the sofa. She wished she could smoke down here. Part of her almost had yesterday. Nathaniel was gone, and so was Natalie, it seemed. No, she had to hope Natalie was coming back. "She needs to get better."

"For that to happen, I have to know what happened to her. What was the start of this? Before the first night, I mean."

"Oh, there was a morning she was at the fridge, asking for meat. I told her I'd make her breakfast and she only ate her sausage. I thought she was being picky."

Margaret tapped her pen against her notebook. Asking a client what happened was much like a doctor dealing with a patient. A patient could already know what they're doing wrong and just needed the right questions to pry it out.

I'm having a rough time breathing, doc.

Well, are you still smoking?

Yup, two packs a day. Why do you ask?

Heather was a proud client. Margaret expected she and her husband were similar in that sense, but her husband died long before Natalie's condition set in, and so never had to experience his resolve being whittled away night after night. Experiences like these could break anyone eventually. Sooner if it was your own child. Right now, Natalie slept upstairs, where she couldn't hurt anyone. That would change by nightfall.

"Heather, I want you to really think hard, back to before it got bad. Did anything strange happen earlier that day? That week? Something out of the ordinary. A place Natalie wouldn't normally go, a person she might've spoken with? Something new or different. It would've given you pause."

Heather sat quiet for a moment. Then her eyes lit up and her mouth twitched. There was an unpleasant thought inside her that demanded it be unleashed, it was plain to see on her face. She worked her lips past it. "The study." She left the sofa.

Margaret hurried to catch up with her at the end of the first-floor hall.

"I only open it up when I'm cleaning." Heather reached a set of double doors, so thin you could punch through them. "I keep it the way he left it. It didn't seem right to move anything."

"Of course."

She reached over the doors and retrieved a small iron key. "We only took a couple things from inside to bury him with, like his favorite hat, a photo of us, you know. Other than that, his study stays locked. Sometimes I dust and vacuum. No one else sets foot inside."

Margaret stepped closer. "Except?"

"I must've forgotten to lock it after I vacuumed last month. I don't know. It's been a rough time. I don't even remember if I closed the doors." Heather slid the key into the lock. "When I passed through the hall again, Natalie was in there." The flimsy doors swung open without a touch.

The air hit Margaret before the sight of Nathaniel's study. It carried a man's stink, even after all these months. It also carried scents of dirt and must and preserving chemicals, of animal hair and wood finish.

And there was a weight in the air. Margaret didn't consider herself any kind of medium, but she expected that after last night's encounter, her body would at least recognize a similar sensation. There was foreboding here, a presence that lived in the space of a dead man, so obvious and disquieting that even a layman like Heather could feel it. It was obvious in the way she shuddered when the doors finished opening. She led the way inside.

Margaret closed the doors of the study behind them. There was a risk that they might lock on their own, perhaps if the Glasgow house was haunted, but she thought not. Only one person here was haunted. Besides, they really were flimsy doors. She didn't want the atmosphere here to go floating around the halls and up the stairs. Better to be mired in it. Let it get to know her.

To the left of the door, she found Nathaniel's desk, where he displayed a fisher that had been handled by a taxidermist. He had also displayed a photo of a hunt. Margaret leaned in for a closer look.

It was a photo of Nathaniel himself, and he looked exactly as his study suggested him to Margaret, the spitting image of an archaic great white hunter, some relic of an imperial century past. He was a stiff-necked, bald-headed man with a sharp, hawkish nose. Margaret half-expected to see a generic safari hat in one hand, but instead he held a hat sewn of golden fur. He wore a white shirt with rolled-up sleeves, brown khakis, and leather boots surely made from some creature he'd killed. Margaret didn't know anything about guns, but Nathaniel's looked big enough to bring down a rhino. Under his boot lay a dead wildebeest.

The man enjoyed his hunting.

The animals of the study told their own bloody story. They were impossible to ignore, with their glass orbs staring from where eyes once stared. There were typical remains that Margaret expected to see in the trophy room of a hunter, like the mounted head of a North American deer, a red fox, a stuffed mallard with its green head and white collar. Then there were more unusual trophies, such as the head of a black bear, the standing fisher on the desk, a wolverine.

And there were exotics, like elephant tusks, a rhino's horn, and the heads of a giraffe, a dingo, and others. Margaret wasn't sure all of these were legal, but the hunter was beyond the law now. Nathaniel Glasgow's pride gazed glassily from the center of the wall that faced opposite the door, where he mounted the heads of a timber wolf, a lioness, a boar far larger than Margaret had ever seen, and a crocodile skin that stretched from wall to wall just beneath the ceiling.

"I know what it looks like," Heather said. "A man this violent out in the world, he must've been violent at home. I shouldn't have told you about his coming home drunk. It paints an unfair picture. He never hurt us. Nate was a hard man, but not a cruel man."

Margaret didn't know enough about him to say she was wrong, but cruel or not, he was merciless. "Where was Natalie?"

Heather pointed to the center of the room. "Right there, on the floor. She was sitting and staring. I didn't pay attention. I just stormed in, grabbed her, and hauled her out." She pressed the heel of her hand against her forehead. "Jesus, I gave her an earful. And for what? She didn't deserve it, just for that. She misses her father. Christ, what's wrong with me?"

"Mrs. Glasgow." Margaret pulled Heather's arms to her sides and looked over her spectacles into Heather's eyes. "It's not worth beating yourself up over. We can't change the past. Believe me, there are plenty of little things I let eat at me at night, but when it comes to helping someone, we have to put all that shit away, pardon my English. Let's help Natalie now, yes?"

Heather nodded. That other thing that was bothering her hounded her eyes and carved her skin into a wrinkled map of countries and states and counties. She lowered her face into Margaret's shoulder and loud sobs quaked through her body.

Margaret held her. "Mrs. Glasgow, did you ever go with your husband on these trips?"

Heather shook her head.

"Besides the animals, did he ever bring anything else back with him? Coins, dolls, masks, the kinds of things—" Margaret cut herself off before she could say, anything that a spirit might attach itself to, as if Heather would know. As if Heather was in the right place of mind to hear such a thing.

"In the desk," Heather managed through a sob. She pulled herself away from Margaret and covered her face. "I'm sorry."

"Please don't be." Many people looked to Margaret for comfort, often after delivery and especially when things went wrong. She never seemed to get any better at it, but she supposed if they kept looking then she couldn't be doing too badly either.

She opened the top drawer of Nathaniel's desk. Stone arrowheads pointed accusingly at her. Ancient coins stared from glass cases. The next drawer held a small mask made of clay, its expression frozen in laughter. The idea that artifacts of another culture carried an inherently demonic presence was ethnocentrism at work, Margaret knew, but something angry could have hitched a ride with Heather's husband. And then poor Natalie.

Margaret glanced back at his photo on the desk. *Greedy, repulsive man. Just what did you bring into your home?*

The photo didn't answer.

"You can stop," Heather said. She seemed to have composed herself.

Margaret looked up. "Stop?"

"You can stop looking. I know what it is. I think I knew it last night when we were talking. It didn't occur to me before, maybe because I'd been hoping it was a demon or a lesion. Can you imagine? Wishing that for my own daughter."

"Mrs. Glasgow—"

"It's Nathaniel."

Margaret gently closed the drawer. She had to choose her tone carefully so as not to sound derisive, especially because she didn't mean to be. "You suspect Nathaniel's ghost?"

"It feels like him. He'd always eat his meat as rare as he could. When he was drunk he'd stomp around the halls like she does every night. That heaviness and strength."

"And the anger?"

Heather lowered her head. "I must've done something wrong. With the funeral or, I don't know. Since then."

"Let's not jump to conclusions," Margaret said. She stepped around the desk and opened the study doors. She was ready to be free of this place. "We have tests for that, too. We can find out if it's Nathaniel through a séance. He's likely to be much less dangerous than a demon."

Heather followed Margaret out of the study. "How long would it take to get one of those ready?"

"A séance? A week, maybe, to bring my contacts together. Maybe by then your dreams will—"

"No." Heather yanked the doors shut and thrust the iron key into the lock. "If you had to get him out of her, how long would it take to be ready? If you knew for certain."

"I could do that myself." Margaret swallowed. "I could do it tonight. But it's a ceremony that draws out whatever's inside her. It'd be dangerous to do that without knowing for certain what it is. We might not be prepared."

"I don't care."

"You can't mean that."

"I don't care about the danger, Ms. Willow, because I care too much about Natalie. We can't keep going like this, waiting and testing." Heather brushed past Margaret, back down the hall, and grasped the stairway banister. "Follow me upstairs. I need to show you something in Natalie's room."

Margaret recoiled as if the sun had set preemptively and Natalie now stalked the halls of the Glasgow house. But the sun hadn't set yet. That would be another couple of hours still. Margaret didn't have an excuse. She followed Heather up the stairs.

Heather wasn't quiet or subtle about opening Natalie's bedroom door. In the day, Natalie was no danger. She was just a young girl in a lot of trouble. The window hung wide open, letting in an autumn breeze, but Heather would have to shut and lock it before nightfall.

Margaret couldn't help but like her room. The walls wore faded magenta paint and parts of them hid behind pencil sketches of different animals. Natalie approached the wilderness with a kinder attitude than her father.

"Come here," Heather said. She stood to one side of the bed.

Natalie lay in a new nightgown. Her skin remained flushed, like last night. A bag of ice lay half-melted beside her head. The air here was cool. It seemed the heat only spread and infected the world after sunset, but Natalie was stuck with it around the clock.

"I get her up to drink every hour or so. She'll use the bathroom." Heather ran her hands through Natalie's damp hair. "Nathaniel inside her is getting stronger, but that's not a physical thing. Natalie, her body, is getting weaker. The force of it, the heat, the ... diet. It's wringing her out, running her ragged. She sleeps through the day, but it's the sleep of nightmares. She's not going to make it much longer. And neither will I."

Margaret could see it. Heather's eyes were bloodshot. The lines on her face were bold and deep.

"I can't lose them both," Heather went on. "And especially not because of each other. Please, Ms. Willow. Margaret. I need your help. I'll do anything, but please, it has to be as soon as possible."

Margaret turned her attention from Heather to the bed. Natalie's breathing was shallow, raspy. She might have had the strongest lungs in the world, but the nights were taking their toll. This thing inside her, Nathaniel or otherwise, was going to dry her out and walk the poor girl to her death. She might've had any number of parasites swimming through her digestive system for all the raw meat she'd consumed. Eleven years of life weren't enough to withstand all this.

Between mother and daughter, everything they were going through, and the fragility of their lives together—what else was Margaret supposed to say?

She clasped her hands together. "I'll be here before dark. But you have to do everything exactly as I say, no matter what."

Heather agreed.

4 Belladonna

None of Margaret's colleagues could appear on short notice. She had expected this. Of course, if she could gather more people last minute, she would've opted for the séance instead. Going solo was another reason not to perform the exorcism yet, if you wanted to call it that. Margaret wouldn't. An exorcism was an expulsion. What she planned to do was more about enticing the intruding presence so that it would manifest outside of the host.

That was what made it so dangerous not to know for certain that Nathaniel was in there.

Heather eyed Margaret's leather bag, now swollen with ritual ingredients. "We're not going to hurt her, are we? I don't think I could hurt her."

Margaret considered a lie, that yes, this would hurt her, and they should wait until Nathaniel's presence could be confirmed. The time for that lie would've been this afternoon, before she surrendered to Heather's pleas.

"Don't worry about Natalie. We're only here to help her. You should worry more about you and me. Natalie already has this thing inside her. When we draw it out, we expose ourselves to it."

"It's only Nate."

"I hope you're right. I really do." Margaret crossed the den and led the way to the double doors of Nathaniel's study. "Is she inside? Is she prepared?"

Heather followed close behind. "I did everything you said." She stepped next to Margaret. "Did we have to wait for sunset?"

"It emerges on its own then. I'm hoping if it's already at the surface, it'll be easier to coax forward." Easier on Natalie, at least. Herself and Heather Glasgow? She didn't think anything would lighten their burden tonight. She turned to Heather. "You don't have to be here for this."

"I suppose not. This isn't my world." Heather pressed open the double doors. "But how could I leave her?"

Natalie lay balled up across the study from the doors, against the wall. Heather had followed Margaret's instructions. She brought Natalie down here, and then laid some of her favorite things around her, some bits of jewelry, a patched-up horsey doll Natalie had probably kept since she was a toddler, and a couple of her most recent drawings. They were to remind her of herself. Hopefully Nathaniel would be more attracted to his own study than his daughter's personal possessions.

Just as important, a glass of salt sat in front of these objects. It was to protect Natalie in case the entity was not her father and might mean to untether itself from her by violence if necessary.

"I only did as instructed," Heather said. "Nothing more. I didn't even restrain her."

"You did perfect." Margaret squeezed Heather's shoulder. "Now let me do my part."

First, there was another dose of salt to add to the room. Margaret closed the double doors, set her bag down, and retrieved a jar filled with white crystals and powder. She shook a line of it along the doorway, and then walked around the center of the study. When she was done, a circle of salt lay between the doors and Natalie.

Heather set her teeth. "Is this witchcraft?"

"These are old practices. Some of them are old as the Roman rites of exorcism. Some, much older." Margaret returned the jar to her bag and drew out five green candles. "You can call them witchcraft if that helps you. A doctor doesn't worry where the methods came from. A doctor wants to heal a patient." She stood the five candles around the circle. "Could I borrow your matchbook, Mrs. Glasgow?"

Heather slipped it from the fold in her dress, where she once also kept cigarettes a lifetime ago, and handed the small white square to Margaret. "Heather. Please."

Margaret lit the five candles. "Thank you, Heather." She returned the matchbook and then returned to her bag. She was nearly done. Next she drew out the largest item, a bundle of cuttings from a spruce tree. "Spruce wood makes smoke. A lot of smoke." She wrestled with her explanation. Heather seemed a sharp woman, but how could you begin to explain to anyone the impermeability of the world? "We need to create what I'd call a vague space. Smoke obscures the senses. We lay that obfuscation between life and death. In smoke and fog, the spirit can roam."

Heather licked her lips. "I don't suppose I can smoke in here myself?"

"Nathaniel made you quit, didn't he? If we present him something he dislikes, I'm not sure we'll succeed."

"It would sure help my nerves."

Margaret used one of the candles to light the spruce ends. It didn't take much to get them going, but she waved her hand over them and helped the smoke to billow. Soon it wafted across the circle and began to rise.

Last of all, Margaret retrieved a clay saucer from the bag and laid a handful of leafy herbs across the top. Then she laid the saucer in the center of the circle. "Belladonna. Better known as deadly nightshade. This is our key."

"Should I get something of his?"

Margaret looked around. "We're surrounded by his things. He should be comfortable here." Peaceful and pliable, Margaret hoped.

"But maybe there's something missing."

"Only if we find out there's something of his that he wants, that's holding him to the world of the living. Otherwise, I don't want to confuse him. If we make a mistake, pick the wrong object, it might remind him of his mortality." Margaret coughed. She never got used to the smoke. "It could repel him. Make him angry, frighten him, send him back into Natalie, turn him from us. We want to draw him out and make him agreeable."

"Finish his business and go." Heather glanced around the room. "He died in his sleep. The autopsy said it was heart failure, what you'd call a natural consequence of living the kind of life he did. I don't know what I could've done better."

"You'll get to ask him in a minute. The sun is almost set."

Margaret already felt that tremble in her hands. Last night she could hardly hold her microphone. Now she was supposed to perform a ceremony, a rushed one. Everything had been such a tumult since then that she hadn't had time to listen through her recordings. Tonight could be the same brand of mistake, of Natalie standing behind her on the stairway of the Glasgow house. Natalie, growling, hungry, strong. Here she would wake up and there would be no doors between them.

Natalie stirred. First she uncurled against the wall. Her back curved and her arms stretched in front of her. The yawn was almost a growl itself.

The smoke clouded Margaret's vision and she had to wipe her spectacles. It was getting almost too thick for the spruce bundle to have made on its own. Nathaniel's study lay mired in a gray cloud, broken only by the gentle light of the branches and the circle of candles. The spruce bundle stood on one end and burned from its top. The fire would take some time to reach the carpet. If the drawing of the spirit took that long, Margaret expected she and Heather would already be dead.

Natalie began to rise. Every movement was deliberate, a subtle stretch of the leg, a gentle rolling in the shoulders. She was in no hurry to stand. Her head turned slow from side to side. The smoke had confused whatever dwelled inside her. There was another growl, but softer now, curious.

"Aren't you supposed to say something?" Heather whispered.

Margaret meant to say something, just that in the heat and intensity, she was having a hard time finding her tongue. It was in there, somewhere.

"Spirit," she said, and then choked on her words. It had to be the smoke. And nerves. And fear. "Spirit, enter our sacred space. Let us speak with you and offer comfort."

Natalie's throat rumbled. She began to pace the far wall. The floor creaked beneath each pensive step. She couldn't see Margaret too well, certainly couldn't smell her, but could she tell the direction of Margaret's voice? Margaret wondered if she should pace as well, but her legs threatened to quit on her at any moment. They were as shaky as her hands.

"Spirit, I know you're here with us." Margaret took a step toward Nathaniel's desk. "Come forward in this place of life and death. Here, we are one." She turned to Heather. "If there's something you want to say to him, say it."

Heather wiped at her eyes. "Nate? It's me. It's Heather. Do you recognize my voice?"

Natalie continued to pace. The smoke thickened, made her harder to see. Margaret could only make out the suggestion of an eleven-year-old girl on the other side of Nathaniel's study.

"Nate, I've missed you." Heather took a step deeper into the room, her foot at the edge of the salt circle. "We both have, Natalie and I. God, it's been hard without you. Some mornings I wake up and forget you're dead, like maybe you're off on one of your hunting trips and you'll be home next week. Then I remember and it's like you've died all over again. Stupid, I know. It gets easier—no, not easier. But each time it happens hurts a little less than the last time."

Margaret thought she saw movement beside Natalie, a leg much thicker than hers that kept in stride. When she paced back, nothing. Margaret wiped her spectacles for the twentieth time since morning. At next glance, there was no mistake. Something walked with Natalie in the smoke.

"But then you started this insanity with Natalie. Nate, she doesn't deserve it. It's destroying her life. Whatever I did wrong, don't take it out on her. Please, tell me what to do to make it right."

Natalie didn't seem to notice her mother or the thing that walked with her. It moved as she moved, a puppeteer and its puppet. For these past weeks, it had been a formless spirit that dwelled in Natalie's flesh, but here in the smoke, with the worlds obscured, it was a creature made manifest, not quite dead, not quite alive, not quite physical, not quite immaterial.

And every time Natalie moved one leg, it moved two. Not quite human, then.

"I'll do anything. But let Natalie go. Let's fix this, like we used to do. Happy family, strong family. Right?"

But it wasn't a demon. It couldn't be a demon, not when the holy water and the crucifix did nothing, so that meant it was something else, but it was not Nathaniel. An entirely different thing. Not Nathaniel.

"Heather, stop!" Margaret snapped.

The growl rattled through Natalie's throat, same as it did last night, and coursed through the walls, across Nathaniel's prizes, and within the sleek form that slid through the smoke, across the circle of salt.

Heather's spine stiffened. "Nate?"

Margaret grasped her arm and pulled her close just as the presence lunged. One of the double doors shattered and the spirit in the smoke doubled back toward the salt circle. Margaret pulled Heather alongside Nathaniel's desk. Another rumble ripped through the study.

Not a growl this time, but a roar.

When the form charged again, Margaret wasn't fast enough. It knocked into the desk and Heather at once. She cried out and tumbled toward the wall across from the door. Margaret fell to one side, out of her way, almost into Natalie, who continued her pacing as if none of this was happening. Margaret turned back toward Nathaniel's desk.

Now she saw it clearly, almost there. Almost alive. Dead, spirit, here it didn't matter. In the smoke, all was one. She'd said so herself. Real, present, dangerous.

The shoulders and back stretched so taut that the hair on its back jutted up like spines. Four legs stood atop Nathaniel's desk, their muscles tensed solid as bone. A tail swung behind the hind legs, long and coated in a bush of hair at the tip. Golden cat eyes stared through the fog, as if they could see clear as day, above a mouth cursed into a black frown. That frown parted and the flesh peeled away from curved, sharp teeth.

The lioness's roar sent the study rumbling again, a quake hard enough to knock Nathaniel's trophies off the walls. Margaret's spectacles trembled off her face. In the ever-worsening haze, she only made out the form by the lioness's golden fur. She was much larger than a lioness looked in photographs. The heat was immense, the oppression of a hot day stalking prey in the grasslands. Some prey animal, unsuspecting, hopeless. Trapped in her gaze.

She turned her cat's eyes to Heather, prone on the floor, who didn't make a sound. Then she stepped off the desk, her maw hanging open.

"No!" Margaret couldn't see, could barely catch her breath, but she could still manage a shriek. "Get me! Here! I'm the one who got away!"

The lioness growled yet again. Her next step passed over Heather's legs.

Margaret almost giggled. Her distraction had worked. And now what? She looked around for one of Nathaniel's hunting rifles, but couldn't see anything and hadn't used one in ten years. And then, would it do any good?

She fumbled behind her for something, anything, an object to thrust at the lioness, and never took her eyes off that golden stare. The fiery spruce might have worked if she could find it. The shattered study door would help clear the smoke, but not fast enough. Her hand found a solid chunk of wood, heavy enough that she could fool herself into believing she might fight off four hundred pounds of muscled predator.

She swiped in front of her. "Spirit, you're not welcome here!"

The lioness's throat quaked. She stepped to one side, into the salt circle. Her back arched, the forelegs outstretched. She was about to pounce.

Margaret shoved her weapon in front of her, now a shield.

The lioness hissed. Margaret hadn't ever heard a sound like that from such a big cat. No, it came from beside her. From Natalie. Margaret turned to her.

Natalie hissed again and tore off toward the wall across from the desk. The lioness kept pace with her, to the edge of the smoke, and then Natalie alone smashed through the window. A much weightier creature hit the ground by the sound of her crash and then took off to places unknown.

Margaret glanced down at her hands. Her vision remained smudged, even with the smoke dissipating, but the form of the trophy in her hands was unmistakable—the lioness head she had seen mounted on the wall this afternoon. If she got in her car, she could chase after them. Letting Natalie alone out there, without her midnight snack at the fridge? Someone was going to get hurt.

Someone was already hurt. Margaret dropped the taxidermied head and rushed to Heather's side. "Mrs.—Heather, are you okay? Can you speak to me?"

Heather groaned. "Am I okay?"

"That's what I asked."

"I don't think so." Heather reached down her side. Her hand came back red. "I think I'm dying."

5 A Shade of Gold

Margaret sat in the waiting room outside the emergency room, her head in her hands. She didn't know what had become of Heather yet. The ambulance took her hours ago and she was already in surgery by the time Margaret arrived. She tried to call Heather's sister, but there was no answer at Alicia's house and she hadn't tried again.

She spent the following hours ruminating on her failure, with intervals of sleep here and there. Morning arrived before any news.

A demon had seemed so obvious until it wasn't. Nathaniel's ghost wasn't a bad guess, for everything Heather had suggested. Margaret had considered other options, other kinds of spirits. With Nathaniel's penchant for world travel, anything was possible.

Margaret hadn't considered possession by animal. She had heard of animal avatars that were welcomed to commune with human hosts as part of religious and spiritual practices. This was different. This was an eleven-year-old girl in the heart of Connecticut, who made the innocent mistake of sitting in her late father's study, likely because she missed him. It wasn't her fault that dead animals lined every nook and cranny of that room.

Which brought Margaret to the recordings. She hadn't had the chance to listen to them until after the ambulance pulled away, after the police finished questioning her, while she decided whether she was going to drive home from the Glasgow house or head to the hospital. Before she listened, the recordings didn't seem like they could tell her much she didn't already know.

She was wrong about that, too. They pushed her to drive to the hospital and warn Heather herself.

"Ms. Margaret Willow?"

Margaret placed her spare spectacles on her face and looked up at a nurse in blue scrubs. Her nametag said Rachel.

"Heather Glasgow is awake," Rachel said. "She's going to make it."

News that should've filled Margaret with ecstasy only gave her the slightest relief. Heather would live. One less thing to feel guilty about.

Rachel led Margaret away from the ER, down another corridor to the post-op room where they had brought Heather Glasgow. "She's only come up from anesthesia minutes ago. We gave her another sedative, and something for her pain because Lord knows she'll need it. You'll only have a few minutes, is what I mean."

"Thank you."

Margaret and Heather needed to have a conversation. Margaret would've liked it later, but in case there was no later, it had to be now. Natalie was missing. Margaret wasn't sure how to help. And then there were the recordings. Heather wouldn't be awake long. Margaret wasn't sure she could say any of this before time ran out.

"Were the two of you at the circus or something?" Rachel asked. "That wound. Some big cat must've done that. A cougar or a lion, right?"

Margaret turned to the open doorway. "I need to talk to Heather. I don't mean to be rude." She stepped into the room, up to Heather's bedside.

Heather lay under a thin sheet. The lioness had gored her left side, under the ribs, likely when they collided beside Nathaniel's desk. Her face was pale, her eyelids heavy.

Margaret leaned over her. "You have your husband's way with animals."

"Don't make me laugh, Ms. Willow. It'll hurt." Heather's hand snatched Margaret's, quick as a snake. The sedative was going to hit her hard. "When they find out what happened, they're going to blame her. Don't let them hurt Natalie."

"I won't if I can help it." Had she guessed at Margaret's uselessness? Had she listened to the recordings herself since last night and hadn't said anything? Margaret doubted that. Now didn't seem the time to tell her.

Heather stared up with warm, wet eyes. "Promise to help her. I'm sorry I rushed it, but it's not her fault. It's her father's, I'm sure of it. That stupid man."

A promise like that was going to be hard to keep at this point. Not making the promise while Heather lay there, her consciousness fading, would've been even harder.

"I promise," Margaret heard herself say. As if she had a choice. Natalie was already deep in a mess. Nothing else Margaret did could make it worse.

"Okay. You promise." Heather's hand let go. "I want to see her draw more animals, Ms. Willow. I want to see her go to high school. I'm parenting for two. I need to see her live her life, and that means she has to live it. Get that thing out of her. Get it out before she kills someone. Before it kills her." Her eyelids slammed shut. "I love her so much."

Margaret stood up from the bed. Heather put it succinctly, didn't she? Get it out of Natalie. Margaret left the hospital bed and found her way back to the waiting room. She could sit there a while longer, but dwelling on her mistakes wasn't going to help Natalie.

There was work to do. Margaret headed for the parking lot and started her car.

The police had been to the Glasgow house, put up their tape, and done some investigating, but no one stood guard in the driveway or at the front door. Had Heather died, things would be different. As it was, this was only an accident with some peculiarities.

Anyone searching for Natalie Glasgow only did so out of concern. She had gone missing after her mother suffered a wild animal attack and was only eleven years old, after all.

Margaret parked on the street, same place she left her car last night. Heather's car sat in the driveway. The broken window of Nathaniel's study faced the back of the house, which meant Natalie had started from the ground there and probably kept going in that direction.

Which made it all the stranger when Margaret approached Heather's car and found Natalie asleep in the back seat. Her feet were black with soil, her nightgown torn on her left sleeve, and a few burs stuck to the same shoulder. Her mouth looked clear, but her reddened fingernails said she might have eaten in the night.

Margaret opened one door, rolled down a window, and closed the door. Best to let Natalie sleep while she decided what to do with her.

It would be smart to call the police. Let them know where Natalie was, where they could take her off the street so she wouldn't hurt anyone else. That was blood on her fingers, under her nails, no doubt about it. A rabbit? A bird? Something larger? Margaret clasped her hands. Something Margaret-sized?

If she called the police, they would bring Natalie to the hospital, where her mother couldn't hide her any longer. Night would come and then Natalie would give them a reason to lock her up. She wouldn't be able to hurt anyone else. She also wouldn't get any better.

Out here, maybe there was a solution to be found. If they detained Natalie, was there a judge in this world who would let Margaret and her colleagues perform some archaic ritual? She doubted there was one who would even let a priest perform an exorcism. The old ways were nonsense in the days of the new ways unless they could be exploited.

Which meant if she called the police, Natalie would spend the rest of her life in an asylum. The lioness would eventually wear her out and kill her from the inside.

Margaret stepped through the unlocked front door and paused in the living room. She looked up at the second-floor stairway. Natalie had spent most of her time in her bedroom throughout this ordeal, but that wasn't where the ordeal began. Margaret headed for the study, where yellow police tape crossed the shattered door. She opened the other door and slipped inside.

The room remained as she left it—the salt circle, the snuffed candles, the blackened bundle of spruce. The saucer remained intact, but the belladonna was nothing but shriveled pulp. A key with a one-time use.

Outside the circle lay the lioness's head on a wooden mount. Nearby, a partial paw print smudged the salt. Margaret supposed that could be misinterpreted for anything, but she'd seen the lioness cross the circle. She was present. Perhaps if not for the smoke she would've been trapped behind lines of salt.

She picked up the head and placed it back on the wall where it had been mounted yesterday. If the lioness wanted anything, it wasn't this head. The head had warded her off. Was the spirit bent on revenge or did the lioness have a stake in this beyond her own demise at the hands of Nathaniel Glasgow?

"Your body." Margaret glanced over the walls. "What does a man do with a lion's body when he only wants the head?"

She imagined in many cases where lions were part of the ecosystem, the lion was eaten, either by hungry people or scavenging animals. A call to the taxidermist wasn't out of the question. She would have to hope he was still in business and that Nathaniel kept his number in a rolodex, perhaps knocked off the desk last night.

A step toward the desk made glass crunch beneath her foot. She leaned back on her heel, expecting to find her spectacles from last night, even more broken than before.

Instead she found the framed photo of Nathaniel, his foot proudly planted on a wildebeest. No wildebeest prize graced the study. Maybe it wasn't impressive enough to him or he couldn't drag it back to the States. Or maybe it was only bait for another hunt. Hence, the photo. It had to be a compulsion for him, a means of mastering the world. He might have expected that when he was gone, the study left intact, that people would step through those double doors and his wife would show them the marvel that was her husband.

Nothing on this Earth that man couldn't find and kill, Heather might say, if she were a different kind of person. Her words to Margaret when they first entered the study told a different story. Heather was embarrassed by this room, afraid it made her husband out to look like something worse than he was.

And she had no idea how bad it was. Margaret knew. She had listened to the recordings. At first they played only snippets of her conversation with Heather from inside Heather's bedroom. Then there was Natalie's door and Natalie herself, and the weight of the lioness she carried through the house.

But there were other sounds. They began with insects in the distance, a foreign-sounding cicada cacophony. It might've sounded normal if this wasn't autumn. There was no rationalizing the other sounds. An elephant's cry. Galloping hooves, maybe gazelle, maybe zebra. A bear, a hissing crocodile, birds of all kinds.

"I don't know why you had such a potent draw," Margaret said to the photograph. "I've never seen it so bad. Everything you killed became a frayed yarn ball of fury, ready to snag anything it touched after you died. Even here, even with me. How can I know I'm not being exposed to any of these poor animals right now?"

A color caught her eye. She peered closer at the photo.

And then she saw it. She saw it, knew that shade of gold, and remembered what Heather told her about it, if it was the same. It had to be the same.

"If I'm right." Margaret set the frame down on the messy floor. "Please, I have to be right this time."

She couldn't leave Natalie to be found. She would have to come with, maybe get some water in her, take her to the restroom at some gas station on the way. They couldn't delay too long. It was morning now, but eventually it would be night again.

Margaret returned to the living room with her bag. Most of what she brought to the Glasgow house last night was useless here now, but she had her own book of numbers and addresses. She picked up the receiver for Heather's rotary phone on the wall and began her calls.

First she called Trish at home and told her she wouldn't make it for supper again, and perhaps not to expect her until morning. She left out the severity of the situation.

Second, Margaret called Alicia again. This time, she answered. Margaret told her not to ask questions, but that she needed information and Heather wasn't in a state to answer. Alicia told her what she needed to know and she told Alicia what hospital to find Heather.

Last, because Margaret couldn't get the recordings out of her head, she gave Alicia instructions, and to either have Heather carry them out after she recovered, or for Alicia to carry them out herself. Someone had to take responsibility and Margaret couldn't be sure she was coming back from this.

"Take everything Nathaniel ever brought to the Glasgow house from afar, pile it up in the backyard, and burn it at sunset." Burning would sanctify. Burning would free anything that shouldn't have been there.

She didn't elaborate. There wasn't time. The sun had been up for too long already.

6 Graveyard Dirt

The sky had grown graciously overcast by the time Margaret arrived at her destination. Natalie stirred in the backseat as they pulled through the front gates, her voice a childlike whimper. Margaret had made sure to give her some water and help her to a gas station restroom on the way, but if she wet the backseat while Margaret worked, so be it. There wasn't time to babysit her.

The car parked on a grassy patch not far from where Alicia had directed. Margaret would've liked nothing more than to sit in the car and talk to Natalie. Easier to make promises than keep them, but if she didn't keep this promise, sitting in this car was going to become lethally unpleasant by nightfall.

"It's illegal," Margaret said. "And sometimes considered blasphemous, but less often than you might think. In your case it won't be immoral. Still." She reached over the seat and caressed Natalie's head. A feverish warmth cooked her skin. "This thing inside you is angry. I can't blame her."

Margaret stepped out of the car, locked it, and grabbed a shovel out of the trunk. Then she stepped across the grass.

Heather said Nathaniel had a favorite hat. Margaret presumed it was the hat in the photograph, a hat the same color as the lioness's fur. Perhaps—hopefully likely—this was what the lioness wanted. And where was that hat? Heather had told Margaret yesterday afternoon.

"Nathaniel Adam Glasgow," Margaret read aloud. The headstone was a black block of clean slate. The dry flowers at its base had been there for maybe a month. "Husband, Father, Traveler. May He Roam Heaven as He Roamed the Earth." She drove the head of the shovel into the earth, grown over with faded grass.

Margaret had performed strange activities and rituals as a midwife, or a witch, whatever you wanted to call her. She'd taken soil from graves before, with permission, and only to help people. Never in her life had she unearthed a grave in a race against the sun.

Nathaniel was a few feet down. Since he died of heart failure and not some horrific accident, Margaret could assume he had an open wake or funeral, which meant the top half of his casket would open on its own. She would only need to dig up his upper half. More of him would have to be dug up just so she could reach that far down, but the soil could form a slope rather than a six-foot long rectangle.

Hours of digging dragged by. Two feet down. Three feet down. The work itself was dull, but time was short. The day dragged on, yet every hour gone was an hour more she wished she had. Now and then, she glanced back at her car. The doors remained closed. Natalie was harmless in the daylight. Margaret wished to get in the car and leave. Her mind hung back in Heather's bedroom, sweating, her nerves on fire, dreading what was to come.

It didn't occur to her until the mid-afternoon that the graveyard was far more dangerous than the Glasgow kitchen. Natalie would awaken with the lioness inside her when the sun set wherever she was, but here in this place of death, there were no promises that the lioness herself wouldn't manifest like in the study.

Margaret grasped a clump of soil from her pile and let the grains sift through her fingers. "Never underestimate the power of graveyard dirt." That power went both ways. She could have used it in her ritual last night, but the belladonna seemed more welcoming to a departed family member. It also gave strength to the presence of the dead.

Gloom overtook the sky prematurely thanks to the overcast. A trick of the light, maybe, but more likely the day would soon end and Margaret wasn't done. She hunched atop the lower half of where the coffin would be and thrust shovelful after shovelful of soil out of the hole. There had to be a bottom to this.

She couldn't help but stand up straight to glance at her car. The windows were beginning to fog. Heather had warned on Margaret's first night that she couldn't set a watch to Natalie's episodes.

"It's just from Natalie's breathing." Margaret returned to digging. She couldn't be too far from Nathaniel's casket. She began to dig in one spot so that she could reach the casket's lid sooner and confirm how far down she still had to go, or how short she was going to fall from finding that hat before—

The car squeaked. Margaret couldn't help herself. She glanced back again.

White mist painted most of the windshield.

Margaret returned to digging. "It's going to be a chilly night. Natalie's body heat is just warming the car." Her tone was dismissive, as if what she said was harmless, but she was painfully right. Natalie's body heat became its own atmosphere at night and it was filling her car as night drew near.

The shovel hit a firm surface. Margaret exhaled so hard it came out as a guffaw. Then she gritted her teeth and growled, and her digging grew frantic. She was close in one spot, so she was close all around that spot. She just needed to clear the coffin's upper half. Another fifty or so shovelfuls, maybe.

Her car squeaked again. Now the windshield and fellow windows were completely clouded up, obscuring the inside like the smoke of burning spruce wood. The sky eased into a quieter, darker hue.

"I won't look again," Margaret promised herself. "That's a promise I'm keeping for me. Natalie, sweetie, please wait. Please."

She plowed her shovel to the side of the casket. Blisters dotted her palms. Her arms weren't willing to dig much longer. That was fine—she didn't have much longer to make them dig. She was beginning to see the perimeter of the casket.

Her tires groaned, the car being jostled from the inside. Natalie's body could manage her bedroom doorknob even with the lioness inside her, but maybe not car door locks. The next sound Margaret heard was a hand or foot or paw breaking one of her back windows.

She kept her mouth shut now, breathing as soft as she could while she continued to dig. The casket lid was almost clear enough to open. If she was quiet, perhaps the lioness would hunt elsewhere in the empty cemetery. Margaret could dig and breathe and sweat in peace.

Sweat. She'd been digging most of the day and sweated through most of it. Her blazer hung from the side of Nathaniel's headstone, a blazer she'd already used to distract Natalie another night. Body and clothing reeked together. The lioness would smell it, sure as she smelled it last night and the night before.

Stiff, dry grass crunched beneath heavy steps.

Margaret fell to her hands and knees and swept at the lid of the casket. One hand fumbled for a latch. A simple, brass-colored clasp held the casket shut on the right side. She tugged, but it wouldn't budge. There wasn't time to figure out how to open it. She stood again, lifted her shovel high, and drove the head down on the lock. The clashing metal sang loud as a dinner bell.

If Natalie drew closer, Margaret didn't hear her now. The lioness could be quiet too, like the other night when she crossed from kitchen to stairs. Wouldn't want to alarm her prey. As if Margaret could crawl out of this hole fast enough to outrun a hungry, undead predator.

Only the ache in her legs and the stinging across her hands kept her from turning to useless jelly. Her fingers clawed at the edge of the casket and thrust it open. The smell hit her strong. She had to press her face into her arm and hide a cough. When she leaned over the open casket again, there was heat across her back. She didn't dare look, not after keeping her promise this far.

Nathaniel had been dead ten months. Long enough to decompose, not long enough to be a skeleton. There was no hat on his head.

A growl rumbled just above. It quaked through Margaret's bones and the dewy bones beneath her. She broke her promise to herself. There was Natalie, standing in her dream-like stupor, the way she stood at the fridge that first night.

And at her side, head leaned down into the grave, stood the lioness, her golden gaze fixed on Margaret. The one who got away twice now. She would pounce tonight. She would feed.

Into the coffin. The thought turned Margaret's stomach, but if she clambered inside with the body and closed the lid, she would be safe until pre-dawn when Natalie's episode passed. The casket had to stand against all the earth. It could resist four hundred pounds of muscle and fury. It had to.

Margaret pressed her hands against Nathaniel's clothes and his chest gave way beneath her. "It's your fault," she said. "You were supposed to have the hat. You did this to your family."

The lioness tensed. Margaret didn't have to look. She could feel those muscles, feel that black frown on the lioness's snout curl open into a hungry maw. Saliva dripped onto the nape of Margaret's neck, into her soiled hair. The lioness was practically alive tonight among the mounds of earth. Perhaps even Margaret had underestimated the power of the graveyard soil to unite the worlds of the living and the dead.

Her hands pawed across Nathaniel, pressed him to the side to make room. The stink made Margaret's head swim. She couldn't pass out here, no matter how exhausted and overwhelmed, not with the lioness above her. Her arm stretched into the lower half of the coffin.

Bristly fur stabbed at the blisters on her palm.

Of course Nathaniel didn't wear the hat on his head. That would have looked crass at the wake and the funeral, as if the man's pride was more important than his family's mourning. The hat was tucked into the side of the casket, gently, lovingly. Margaret's fingers seized it and tore back from inside the casket.

"I have it!" she snapped. She saw it for the first time as she sat up. That beautiful golden color, twisted into an ugly little round hat, the hair trailing down a little as if it was a coonskin cap made of lion.

On the slope of soil, the lioness hunched her back. About to strike. About to maul.

Margaret forced herself to stand. She thrust the hat at the lioness's face. That golden gaze shined beyond the hat. The lioness didn't understand. Her spirit obeyed instinct, and that instinct said hunt and feed, nothing more.

"This is what you wanted. Take it." Margaret stumbled over the open casket. She was about to die. She knew it sure as the lioness knew she was about to eat. This wasn't that night in the kitchen with Natalie and the crucifix, when untold possibilities stirred in the darkness. This was a surety. She owed a hundred apologies and wouldn't have the chance to give a single one.

She pressed the hat only inches from the lioness's face. The lioness inhaled its scent and neither she nor Margaret knew the graveyard anymore.

All she knows is the heat today.

It is immense. It is greater than hunger. She cannot wait for the others to return. She must drink. It is not a hunt. She is sloppy, but she only understands this later.

At the watering hole, the prey-beasts continue to drink despite her presence. She is not close, but not far. She is not interested in them and they know it. If one of the pride can be seen, then she is not a threat. If she wished to be a threat, she would not be seen. Always fear one of the pride that is unseen, as if she is always there.

One creature does not respect the ways of the watering hole. It is not a starving hyena and not an elephant in heatstroke. It is a man-beast. She has seen his kind before and knows the terrible fire and earth they spit from afar. He sees all there is to see at the watering hole, or so he thinks. He sees her, yes. He does not see her see him.

When he tries to sneak, when he tries to kill too close, she is on him. She comes to drink. Had he come to drink, she would have let him, but he comes to kill. So she must kill.

Or try to. The man-beast knows her kind. His fire and earth pierce her foreleg when she pounces at him. Her claw rips his chest, her teeth find his arm. Another peal of thunder puts his fire into her low places. This tells her to leave, but not before she's taken a small piece from one limb. Then she disappears into the brush, her thirst not sated, her blood sating the thirst of the earth. She is dying.

She wants to go home. To wander is more important, to not lead the man-beast back to her. She believes the man-beast to be like one of the pride in this, to chase the weary, the injured, the sick across the grasses, to devour the prey.

The man-beast is different. She learns this only when her long, wayward travel finds her home. By then, she is weak with lost blood, with thirst. The sun above is merciless. Merciless as the man-beast.

The man-beast did not follow her trail of blood, but instead found the path she took to reach the watering hole and followed it to where she came from. To home. To where she left her three small ones.

They are missing.

If the man-beast's fire was not killing her, she believes she might stay. Lost cubs can be replaced if their mother lives. Except she does not want to replace them. They were hers. They were the first she had and now the last. The male she made them with was young and soon driven from the pride by a stranger. Many nights she hid her small ones from this strange male. She took great pain to keep them alive in this world.

She cannot let them go. So, she begins to walk. The man-beast can track. She can track, too. She tracks his steps and the trails of the monstrous wheeled creatures that the man-beasts ride. He leads her through the grass and into a place where the man-beasts gather. There are young she can easily feed on, but she is not here for feeding. She is here for revenge.

The other man-beasts cry out when she enters their nest. The man-beast who stole her young hears the warning, is expecting her. He readies to spit fire and earth, the same that is killing her but has not killed her yet.

Again, she does not understand the ways of the man-beasts. They are not like the prey-beasts, and most importantly, they are not like the pride.

It is her small ones who give her pause. It is her small ones who kill her. They lay on a table. The man-beast has killed them.

If she understood the language of the man-beasts, she would hear that they had no intent to kill her small ones. They want cubs alive. There was an accident. A fall, because the man-beast who is killing her was too weak to carry the bag he stowed them in. She cannot comprehend. There is only heat and rage, thirst and starvation, and deep inside, an emotion she can barely understand. All those nights she protected them, only for their lives to end in this. She wants a greater destiny for her young. Too late. All for nothing.

The man-beast erupts and she feels the fire and earth again, this time through her neck. Blood cakes the fur down her limbs, her belly, and now it crosses her face. She watches the small ones' faces. They are the last thing she sees in the living world.

And what comes after is hunger, fear, and hatred. She can see nothing else.

***

The lioness retreated from the edge of the hole. Nathaniel's cap lay idle in the soil. The lioness growled low. Three mewling throats answered her. Where there were once only four legs, now three lion cubs circled and nuzzled.

Margaret stood steady and cautious. She remained fixed under that golden gaze, but the force of it slackened. The lioness looked confused, as if she hadn't known what she was doing, hadn't even remembered she birthed little ones or what happened to them when their mother crossed paths with Nathaniel Glasgow.

Natalie moaned. Margaret clambered up out of the hole just in time to catch her before she went careening into her father's grave. She pulled Natalie back from the edge, across the soil mounds, and held onto her tight.

Natalie nestled her face into Margaret's chest and began to cry. They were the same racking sobs as her mother.

"It's alright," Margaret whispered. "Everything's okay now. You're safe. Let it out. Good girl. You'll be okay." Over and over, as many times as Natalie needed to hear it, as many times as Margaret could say it. She rocked Natalie back and forth.

Her attention returned to the lioness and her cubs.

The lioness finally turned from her and Natalie. She pressed her face against each of her cubs and breathed deep the scent of them. They purred beneath her, chased at each other, no memory of what had happened to them.

Margaret hoped the same for Natalie.

The lioness uttered a rumbling purr and ushered the cubs ahead of her. They began to pad along, still playing, but headed east. Their mother brought up the rear, where she could keep an eye on them. Tonight and last night, she stalked with each step, a predator on the hunt. Now she strolled peaceably, her long tail swatting back and forth.

Behind her, she dragged a strip of fleshy material the way a hurried shoe might drag an unnoticed errant strip of toilet paper out of the restroom.

Margaret grasped Natalie's head tight to her chest in case the girl stopped crying and tried to look. She couldn't have her seeing this.

It was Nathaniel Glasgow. Part of him. No muscle, no inner tissue, no bones. He was only a skin, dragged by his leg at the hind foot of the lioness, an unmoving, powerless shadow.

Almost all skin, a hide stripped from a body. On his face, most of it caved-in where a skull would have been in life, to the side of his now-shriveled hawkish nose, Nathaniel still had one wide eye. It looked this way and that, alert and pleading. No other part of him could move. It fixed a desperate stare on Margaret, or maybe on sobbing Natalie, but that was all it could do. Glance and stare and be dragged by the lioness.

Margaret stared back at him. He certainly wanted help. It was outside her power to give. Everything he killed became a frayed yarn ball of fury, ready to snag anything it touched after he died.

Perhaps even himself.

She watched his tearful eye until the lioness pulled him too far away in the dark to be seen. Her golden visage remained a moment longer, but then that, too, faded into the darkness with her three cubs.

A cool breeze set in across the graveyard and Natalie began to shiver in Margaret's arms.

It was going to be a chilly night.

WELCOME TO ENGLAND

March 1981

The overhead hanging lamp and the round table formed a small island in the dark kitchen. Bleary-eyed, with spectacles set on the wooden surface of scratches and condensation circles, a seated figure could imagine the table were floating in the blackness of space, with dust motes for stars and emptiness stretching for countless miles around.

It was easier to think of herself as simply *the seated figure* than as Margaret Willow. If she could stop being herself for a little while, just a shape of tissue, organs, and bones seated on a wooden chair over swirl-patterned linoleum on this island in outer space, then maybe she could get some sleep. No identity, no thoughts. A living thing, plainer than an animal, only a system of processes.

But what if nightmares were part of the process? A dream was the brain working out its troubles. Small wonder she was staying up. She shouldn't have to do work in her sleep.

"Maggie?"

Margaret fished her spectacles from the table's surface and slid them onto her ears and nose as Trish faded in from the night sky. Or maybe the downstairs hallway.

"What are you doing sitting in the dark, love?" Trish laid a gentle hand on Margaret's forehead. "Are you feeling unwell? I should make you a cup of tea."

Margaret wasn't going to argue. She was sorry she'd left the bed so empty that Trish felt her absence in the depths of sleep and had to get up to check on her. Helping Trish to make the tea was a non-starter; it was a one-woman job. Margaret could only sit and wait until Trish carried two steaming mugs to the table, laid them out, and sat on the far side of Margaret's island in outer space.

"You could have turned on the light," Margaret said, trying to be helpful.

"I've made tea in the gloom before," Trish said. "My parents' bedroom was across from the kitchen back in London. The light would've woken them."

"Like I've woken you."

"None of that." Trish swirled a teaspoon through the green-honey water of her mug. "Tell me, what's the matter?"

Even with Trish in the kitchen, Margaret could have continued pretending she was a mere system of processes. But to answer questions? That was another aspect of humanity entirely, from the reactive thoughtless answers of a small child to the overthought grimness Margaret sometimes offered.

"It's a long drive to Manhattan," she said at last. "You have that conference in the morning."

"But right now, I have you," Trish said, determined.

Her teaspoon scraped the mug's rim, reminding Margaret of a Tibetan singing bowl, a séance, a memory of Hope Magnussen. Except Hope wasn't the bad dream keeping Margaret up tonight.

"It isn't any one thing," Margaret said. "I wish it was. Then I'd know how to examine it and step away." She paused, adjusting her spectacles, and realized she hadn't touched her tea yet, not even to lace it with sugar. "Everything is bothering me. All the things I've seen. The world is tender. We have to be careful with it. Especially the parts we don't understand. Do you know how bad it has to be for someone ordinary like me to feel it in the air? It happens sometimes."

"I know there's a lot I don't know," Trish said. "You'd be surprised."

Margaret swirled her teaspoon against her mug. The scraping really sounded nothing like a singing bowl, but her ears and nerves couldn't shake the reminder.

The kitchen's darkness was no longer a blessing of isolation. Margaret had created a liminal space in her own home, and from the unseen stretches of the kitchen, the house, anything might emerge. A ghost. A memory.

"My mother came to England a couple of years ahead of Independence," Trish said. "While I was still inside her. Not the best timing with the war, but it was coming to an end, and there we were."

Margaret smiled across the table and was about to say she remembered this.

But Trish's tone became grave. "Still, she expected me, and later my brother and sister, to have her memories. To her, India was real, and England was an uncomfortable dream we would someday wake up from. And because it was a dream, that meant it couldn't exactly hurt you. At least not with the dream's memories."

Margaret sipped her tea to hide a scowl, not wanting to interrupt Trish's train of thought. She'd never heard Trish talk this way. The world's facets had always been tactile for her, one reason Margaret wasn't supposed to bring her otherworldly work home.

"I was nine when the first boy went missing from our pocket of the city," Trish said. "Children went missing in the usual way, of course, but this was different. There was a change in the air. No one talked about it, but everyone felt it. He was playing at a sidewalk corner, and then he wasn't. My mother acted like it was nothing, said we shouldn't mind neighborhood chatter. She was partly right—I heard talk that his parents were forgetting everything about him. That they did away with him. Nasty rumors.

"Word changed when another boy vanished. That same feeling caught in the air, nothing you could describe, not an odor or a draft. Like a humidity, settled onto you. And when the third boy went missing, the chatter about blaming the parents went away, and out crept other rumors. A predator, certainly.

"But children have their own rumors, the run-off from the adults mixed with that colorful childhood imagination. A boy I knew then, Charlie Fitz, he was the first to mention the 'low-street lady. He wouldn't tell us where he heard about her, maybe from a lot of gossipers, maybe another child. I don't know. His word had it that she was a bony thing, all edges and slender features, and wearing a fuzzy green coat too big and rich for her. He said she crawled out from the basement windows beneath one of the low-level flats, and if she latched her fingers around your ankle, she'd drag you underground in a blink. Like you were never there.

"The boys would make a game of it, daring each other to stand on street corners, all rhyming taunts for the 'low-street lady while we girls had a laugh watching them from across the lane. We knew it was serious, and the game was wrong, but we had to laugh, had to pretend it wasn't happening, or else we'd have to scream.

"I didn't believe about the lady, of course. At least, I mostly didn't believe it." Trish cradled her mug between both hands as if her fingers had forgotten the touch of warmth. "Still, what you believe in the day changes at night. And between myself and my siblings, there was no warning of what to expect of England's dreams, and even the stories we heard—they were about the countryside. Not the city. It was like a fairy story that way.

"But belief changes for cities, too. In the day, it understands itself, believes it's made up of flats and smog and rubbish. But at night, it dreams of when it was wild. And no matter how much time has passed since that wildness, the memory won't slough easily away.

"After fourteen months and six vanished children, Charlie Fitz himself was the last. Gone while playing his fool game.

"Shortly after, someone found that wild memory. It looked like a basement." Trish briefly pursed her lips. "And it looked like the countryside. I saw it only for a moment, jostling with other children, nudging between neighbors' hips, and the coppers were shouting for everyone to keep back. I saw anyway. I looked through that basement window for only a blink, but I saw it.

"There was a dirt floor underneath a three-story of flats, where a wart of earth swelled up the size of your car. They told us later it was a gas pocket, formed from a leak, dangerous, but that didn't make sense with what I saw.

"There was a hole in the wart. Its mouth was grown round with toadstools, and the middle was blacker than your pupil. I've never seen a darkness like that. Like the light was afraid of it. And the size—big enough for one of those skinny lads to slip inside. Or be dragged."

Trish slid her hands from her mug. "I never learned any more about what might've happened, or what it might've been, or whether the children had been taken down that hole. The police cordoned off the basement that afternoon. Within a week, city administration had emptied and demolished the building. Built new flats on top. Pretended the whole thing never happened, like they were us little girls across the street, having a laugh so not to scream.

"No more children vanished, at least not in a way that left that feeling in the air. Only the usual kind of travesty. If I'd been braver, I would have snuck in there one night while it was cordoned off and had more story to tell. But it's only a lingering question mark now."

Margaret's voice came shaky. "If you'd been braver, you might not be sitting here."

"True," Trish said, a small smile crossing her lips. "I've never told anyone about that. Maybe because I didn't think they'd understand. Not even you. But it's lighter letting it out. Just a little. Especially at night. It's the right time to let it out of me."

She waited in case Margaret had anything else to say, but she was lost for words.

That only made Trish smile harder. "I told you you'd be surprised."

She drank from her mug again, finishing her tea, and then carried it to the sink, still cloaked in the kitchen's gloom.

A Trish-shaped absence had never dawned on Margaret before. Was this how Trish felt when Margaret took on one of her investigations? Especially those rare occasions when it was a genuine otherworldly occurrence, and more so during those rarer dangerous ones? Margaret had demanded more dedication from herself since that evening when Hope Magnussen took her own life. Too many times, Margaret had wondered if she was doing enough.

And yet for all the uncertainty she'd faced, she'd poured much worse uncertainty into Trish, wondering whether Margaret's next investigation would turn out to be a hoax, a mistake, or a threat.

Or if Margaret would come home at all.

Trish once more faded in from the darkness, now at Margaret's side. Her thin hands encircled Margaret's wrist.

"Trish," Margaret breathed. "I'm so—"

The apology broke apart as Trish raised her voice. "Margaret Willow is tender, don't you think?" she asked. "We have to be careful with her. Especially the parts we don't understand, those lingering question marks." She raised Margaret's hand to her mouth and kissed her warm palm. "But we might understand a little more than she believes. Just a little."

She flashed a wink and then drew Margaret out of her seat, where they held each other in the lit island within the kitchen's outer space. Dust motes briefly echoed floating stars again.

And then Trish led Margaret away from the table, and her half-finished mug of tea. The hanging lamp winked out behind them.

TRIP HOUSE

October 1983

The black street glistened with fresh raindrops and puddles where Natalie Glasgow stood digging through her swollen purse. Damp odors climbed from the sidewalk, and she needed smoke to kill them.

"Do you got a lighter?" she asked. She quit thrashing at her compact mirror and tampons and looked to Basil Trent beside her.

"Nope," he said, but he patted his letterman jacket anyway as if a lighter might materialize within.

Natalie's fingers scraped the belly of her purse, tucking sediment under her nails. Her forefinger stroked a plastic side, and at last she drew her small blue lighter to the cigarette dangling from her lips.

"It's that important?" Basil asked.

"I can't smoke at home," Natalie said, sucking in a flood of ashen smells. Better than rain.

Basil's cheeks were red with the October chill. "But doesn't your mom?"

"Depends on her mood." Natalie slipped the lighter into the pocket of her denim jacket. She didn't want to lose it again inside her abyssal purse.

"What about you?" Basil asked.

"I'm in a mood." A thin trail of smoke slid from Natalie's lips, mixing with her cloudy breath.

Basil nodded. "Okay, but—"

"Bass, can you be quiet for thirty seconds?" Natalie asked.

She watched him nod again. Good enough. She planted one sneaker against the wet brick wall behind her and leaned her head back against it, eyes closed, puffing smoke toward the starless night sky, feeling the drip of raindrops from the awning overhead into her cloudy, light hair. It didn't used to be this color when she was younger, but it had grown furious and golden shortly before she turned twelve, like lion fur.

Her temper was like that, too. Basil didn't deserve it.

She sighed a thick mist. "This season is bad for me. I'm always pissy."

Basil nodded yet again, his brown eyes giving a blank look. "Any reason?" he asked.

"My dad died in November a few years ago," Natalie said. "And something happened to me the next September. So, October gets weird for me, sandwiched in between. Especially since it's my birthday."

Basil's eyes widened. "Whoa, seriously? Happy birthday."

He was such a dope, but he meant well. Natalie smiled for him. One thing she had learned from her mother—most boys and men were satisfied with a smile.

"Yeah," she said. "Sweet sixteen."

"We should celebrate," Basil said.

"That's why we're out here, doofus." Natalie took one last drag from her cigarette, tossed it down, and squashed it under her sneaker heel. "I want to see the Trip House."

She crossed the street, where rain-streaked plastic sheets dribbled down another brick wall in broad translucent tongues. Squat and flat-roofed, it had once been the building adjoined to a community pool, with locker rooms, showers, bathroom stalls, and cleaning equipment.

But the powers that be had filled the pool with concrete when Natalie was little and built a bigger one elsewhere in town. There had been no purpose to this pool house for years.

Until earlier this month when two boys planted themselves in steel folding chairs to either side of the entrance and propped up a white handmade sign charging admission to the Trip House.

Other kids smoked, drank, and chatted on the grass. Most were Natalie's age, but here and there stood a college kid. The boys at the entrance were only high school freshmen, both pale and gangly. They would be easy to muscle past for anyone who wanted, and Natalie guessed only the power of entrepreneurship and the laziness of this town kept them from getting cheated or robbed. A glass pickle jar sat between them, its inside gleaming with deposited coins.

"Dollar-fifty gets you in," the taller one said.

"Why's it called that?" Natalie asked. "Trip House."

"You'll see."

"No, Marty, sell it," the shorter boy said. He looked ready for a growth spurt any day now. "Because it's a trip."

Natalie scrounged through her belongings again, found her soft coin purse, and plucked out six quarters. She was about to drop them in the pickle jar when Basil's hand closed on her shoulder.

"Hey," Basil said. "You don't want to catch a movie or something?"

Natalie scrunched her nose, hawkish like her father's. "How's that anything special? We can do that anytime. I only get a birthday once a year."

"Just that—" Basil rubbed the back of his neck. "I'm not supposed to go into places like that."

"Then wait outside," Natalie said.

A stiff wind slid around her, wafting raindrops from the grass and crinkling the Trip House's plastic sheeting. The narrow entryway stood black against the worn-out bricks. Natalie couldn't see any light inside, but others had gone in without complaint. And if she didn't like it, she could leave. Her fist again reached for the pickle jar.

"It's really your birthday?" the shorter boy asked. He studied Natalie's eyes and then pushed her coin-stuffed fist away with a clammy hand. "On the house, tonight only."

Marty turned to him. "Shane, the fuck?"

But Shane chopped the air, silencing his business partner. A genuine smile slid across Natalie's lips. She hoped Basil didn't see, and if he did, that he couldn't tell the difference between the fake and the real. She slid the quarters back into her purse and approached the Trip House's slender entrance.

"Not for too long," Shane said.

"Why?" Natalie asked, another gust billowing her hair.

Marty snickered. "Stay too long, and you'll never come back."

It was forever, and it was ten minutes, and it wasn't enough time when the boys called for Natalie to leave the Trip House. But there was so much more to it than its bricks and plastic suggested.

"Thought we'd have to drag you out," Shane said, sounding relieved.

Natalie's hair had somehow puffed from a peaceful day's cloud into a sky-swallowing thunderstorm. Her cheeks were pale and dotted with sweat. Meager applause burst from the crowd, plus a couple shouts of "Woo!" by the idling kids. Natalie exhaled a surprised laugh.

Had any of these kids stepped inside? Did they share the contradictory ease and exhilaration of the Trip House, a wonder Natalie hadn't felt since she was a child?

She stood panting beside Shane's chair. "When can I go back in? Tomorrow?"

Shane licked his chapped lips. "Should wait a day. To be safe."

"Tomorrow night," Marty said.

Natalie gave a nod. "Tomorrow night."

Natalie found the picture window glowing bright when Basil dropped her off at home. She considered sneaking in through the outside door of her father's study, but she would have to pass through the living room to get to the rest of the house anyway, and she refused to sleep there even now that Heather had turned it into a storage room. The taxidermized animals were gone, burned by Aunt Alicia years ago and replaced by dusty books and cardboard boxes full of neglected souvenirs.

Heather could have lurked in the dark, waiting to catch Natalie, but she was never one to ambush. Natalie wouldn't disrespect her forwardness by creeping in like prey.

She found her mother sitting on the stairs with a magazine. "Happy birthday, Nat."

"Ha—" Natalie started to say *Happy birthday* in return as if this were an ordinary evening greeting and then caught herself. "Hi, Mom."

"Out late," Heather said, turning a crinkly page.

"Home before curfew." Natalie hung her denim jacket on the coatrack and started for the stairs. Across the living room, a wall clock showed quarter to eleven. "I still had a few minutes."

"But it's your birthday. I thought—" Heather set down the magazine. She looked itchy for a cigarette but refused to smoke in the house. "It doesn't matter what I think."

"I wanted to see Bass." Half true. Natalie had wanted Basil to drive her to the Trip House. No one else would.

Heather studied her fingernails. "Are you being careful?"

"Mom, it isn't that." Natalie tried to cool the annoyance from her voice. If she let it take over, it would simmer into anger and then boil into a roar. "You know how it is. I need to get out at night."

"You could prowl the back yard," Heather said.

Natalie's fingers twitched. She had been a night owl since she turned twelve, nights made her restless, but the back yard offered too little space for roaming.

"You promised I'd see better grades this marking period," Heather went on. "If I don't, you won't be going out anymore."

"The C's and D's aren't from going out," Natalie said. "I'm just tired."

"That's what I mean, Nat. You need sleep."

"Not that kind of tired." Natalie bristled. "And you know what I mean. You feel it too."

Heather only stared until Natalie slid around her and climbed the steps. She could never tell anymore whether or not her mother would come say good night to her, and she tried not to worry about it. Heather could say it, and then Natalie would be up for hours after that trying to keep the night good when sleep wouldn't come. Sometimes she stared at the ceiling in the dark, begging for dreams while an anxious twinge told her she should be out wandering the tree-dotted neighborhood, searching for—something.

But that twinge never told her what to find. It was an empty want, a hunted absence. She felt the same in her bedroom, her animal drawings replaced by band posters and Basil's Polaroids. It was not an absence to be filled, more like the absence was doing the filling up, and it left no room for anything real.

But the Trip House was different. Natalie's room might have been empty, but the Trip House was full and thriving. She could still feel its delicate touch on her skin, its breath in her hair, the calm in her nerves.

And the stars—more beautiful than the sky outside. She could hardly wait to go back.

"I told her she needed sleep, even though I don't believe it," Heather said. "And then she says, *Not that kind of tired. You know what I mean. You feel it too.* That was over a week ago, and she's barely spoken to me since. I mean, Christ, is she sixteen or thirty-six?"

Margaret Willow sipped from her mug of black coffee and refused to look back at the shut study doors. While she had kept visiting the Glasgow house during the period of Heather's and Natalie's parallel recoveries back in 1979, she'd since only called Heather once a year to check in. That was the major failing among her fellow experts. They rarely followed up with families and individuals to ensure against a relapse of haunted sensations, furtive symptoms, general trauma, or even the attraction of another supernatural presence.

Now Margaret wondered if annual phone calls were enough. Natalie's mood had crashed, but only toward ordinary adolescent chaos. Nothing to do with her encounter at age eleven, or at least that was how it had sounded over the phone. Heather seemed to think differently when she invited Margaret over this afternoon.

They sat in the living room, Margaret on the couch and Heather having taken over her late husband's red leather chair. The arms were worn with the years.

"A sixteen-year-old should want a birthday party," Heather said. "She shouldn't stay up until ungodly hours of the night, and sleep through classes, and is it too much to ask her to wait on this behavior until she's out of the house? Or at least have better taste in boys than that Basil kid in his red truck."

"Did you, at her age?" Margaret asked.

"Of course not. I'm sure my mother felt the same, but we were best friends." Heather leaned back with a huff. "I know Natalie's young. And I know it's different. She can't help that. I just hoped at least that one thing could be normal for us. Now she's like a stranger in my house. Like—" Her nervous hands tugged the hem of her white blouse. "Nothing would have gotten into her again, would it? Not like before?"

There it was. That threat of relapse. Margaret folded her hands over her lap. "I doubt it's anything scarier in her than hormones."

Heather draped her forearm over the chair's side with two fingers splayed as if clutching an invisible cigarette. The past four years had dragged at her, streaking premature gray hairs across her scalp and wearing lines through the whites of her eyes.

Margaret wondered if time had taken the same toll on her. She never felt any different, always her stocky self, always wearing her blazers and slacks, forever cutting her hair short, diving into situations most people would either ignore or avoid or cross themselves over. Years were more mathematical than physical, even if her muscles and bones shared a less optimistic opinion and her spectacles wore thicker glass than before.

But she and Trish didn't have children. That likely made a difference.

Margaret reached from the couch and clutched Heather's other hand. "I'm sorry, Heather. I should have visited sooner."

"Oh, you have your own life," Heather said, annoyed with herself. Her eyes flicked past Margaret, to the study perhaps, and then back. "Maybe you remember, the county spent two weeks searching the area for an imaginary cougar. Nothing but pawprints too large for a mountain lion. Some nights I go to bed thinking it didn't happen, and then in the morning, in the shower, I wash my belly and feel the scars. Almost a c-section without a birth. They'll never go away completely. Natalie's scars are permanent, too, but different.

You can see that thing in her hair color, the way her eyes get when she looks at you wrong. Sometimes you feel it in her at night."

"The spirit's gone," Margaret said. "I promise you, I saw her."

Heather shifted in her seat. "But the fact that it was there—that past will *always* be there. I can't make it so it was never there."

Margaret understood. She had been lucky to escape Natalie's ordeal with only ravaged nerves, but occasional nightmares reminded her of the frantic graveyard digging and the momentary vision of sunbaked grasslands when she briefly forgot she was human.

"I know you're right," Heather said, shifting again like she couldn't seem to wear her impression into the chair. "But isn't it possible Natalie could attract something else? Or be attracted to it? The way you can be more vulnerable to one disease if you catch another? I know the world is fucking weird, and I remember you told Alicia to burn the other animals from Nate's study. Like he'd caught more than their bodies. Natalie could be like that, couldn't she?"

Margaret couldn't keep from nodding. She had always told Heather the truth, and she wasn't going to change that now. Yes, subsequent attractions were possible. Sometimes the living victim, sometimes a dead relative like Nathaniel Glasgow, but either way, certain souls were like spiritual thornbushes, always catching scraps of passing forces.

"There's a pool house on the far side of town." Heather's dangling hand curled into a fist. "Kids call it the Trip House. She's been going there nearly every night for a week and a half now. I wouldn't have found out, but her boyfriend's a clear window when it comes to secrets. Something about that place is wrong for her. You can tell me it's college boys giving her beer, and I hope so because then I can ground her for it instead of scaring myself half to death thinking what I'm feeling is right."

"What are you feeling?" Margaret asked.

"It's too perfect," Heather said, a wisp of desperation in her voice. "That doesn't make sense, but it's true. And after I came home from there, I had nightmares. Blank dreams, full of nothing. Maybe that's why Natalie doesn't want to sleep."

She slumped over her knees and clasped her hands. Sudden dread pulled Margaret away, anxious over the sense that Heather was praying to her.

"Can you help me again?" Heather asked. "I want to turn out ridiculous and paranoid. But really, I *need* to know what the hell my daughter's doing in that place."

***

Margaret reached the Trip House a few minutes after noon. She wouldn't ordinarily have been able to jump right into following up, but she'd already kept Heather waiting a few days, and Heather had taken off work specifically to talk with Margaret. The least she could do was drive across town.

Pale sunlight reflected off the plastic sheets covering the pool house's windows and scarred brick. A burr-coated blanket hung from two nails over a black doorway, flapping in the wind as Margaret approached with dead leaves clinging to its frayed bottom. The boys who'd pronounced themselves the doorway's guardians likely thought even a flimsy obstacle would deter the curious during the day.

Margaret tore the blanket down with one hand and carried her Panasonic tape recorder inside with the other. It was a flat beige square with a black-eyed audio cassette within, the buttons jutting like square teeth, each labeled Record, Rewind, Fast-Forward, Play, Stop, and Eject.

Scant sunlight broke through the filthy plastic sheeting, leaving the Trip House hidden in a murky gloom. While Margaret waited on the concrete floor for her eyes to adjust, she hugged the Panasonic to her thigh at the entrance and pressed Record and Play with a heavy *thunk* to start the tape moving.

Darkness molded into a front desk atop a concrete floor. Cubby holes dotted the wall behind it, where the building opened into hallways on either side. Margaret followed one, her footsteps clacking into a changing room where tiled flooring cut into aisles of cabinet-sized lockers. A bathroom lurked beyond, and then another short hall where the building again became a single space. To the left of both changing room entrances, a dark corridor led toward a boiler room and supply closet. To the right, Margaret found the back exit to the pool, chained and padlocked shut.

She kept her microphone aimed ahead at all times, but she saw nothing strange. Or anything dirty, either. No shattered beer bottles, no graffiti, no food packaging, no torn condom wrappers or used condoms, no weed roaches, not even a cigarette butt.

The building was pristine. High school and college kids visited, but they must've held a respect for this place.

As if they loved the Trip House.

After circling the interior for another few minutes, Margaret drifted back outside, where the crisp October sunlight glared across her spectacles. If there was nothing to see in the pool house, was there anything to hear? She braced the tape recorder against her hip to hit Stop, then Rewind, and then Play.

Nothing. The cassette threaded black tape from one eye to the other, but silence played from the recorder's speaker even at full volume. Margaret shook her head and hit Stop again. What more could she expect from an empty building?

Something, she thought. *Anything. An insect, a cardboard box, a carving on the wall.*

But there was nothing. The walls were thin in places due to neglect, but no one had desecrated them, as if worried even the slightest violence might break the plaster, and then the entire Trip House might follow.

The wind batted Margaret's hair into her face and muffled the sounds of distant cars and machines. She would have to give the tape an aural shake with her home equipment and listen to what jangled loose.

"Looking to see the Trip House?" a scratchy voice asked.

A man maybe Margaret's age strolled close in a brown coat, his face hardened with mild sunburn and the scales of watching half a century crawl past. One hand clutched a brown paper bag with the lip of a glass bottle sticking out.

Margaret cocked her head at the pool house. "Isn't this the one?"

The man grinned yellow teeth as he passed her by. "Only at night," he said. "It's a different animal at night."

"At night, then," Margaret said. She thanked him and crossed the street to her car.

An abandoned pool house by day, a strange attraction after sunset. Why had Margaret expected any differently? Of course the Trip House was a different animal at night.

So was the world.

Natalie always waited for dark to leave the house. Her mother misunderstood, thought she meant to be sneaking out, but really it took the sky purpling with sunset for her to find that nocturnal energy. The sensation hit hardest in autumn, and tonight she heard it whispering in her ears. *See me, I miss you, I love you.*

No, that wasn't the night calling. That was the Trip House.

She started downstairs a few minutes past nine, aiming to reach the driveway's end before Basil was supposed to appear at a quarter after. He'd shown up almost every night, even after Heather put a scare in him. Natalie would offer a smile for his loyalty, maybe a kiss if he didn't talk her ear off with suggestions of going anywhere but the Trip House.

Ice crawled into Natalie's heart and down her legs, freezing her on the steps—she wasn't alone. A figure took up one of the living room seats, nestled in the dark. Waiting for her.

She'd once found her father like this. He had come home after midnight from one of his trips abroad, and though she and her mother were used to hearing him stomp around on nights like that, this time he was either too courteous, tired, or drunk to bother with the stairs. Natalie had come down, she couldn't remember why anymore, but the meager light creeping from the kitchen had cast him in silhouette, sitting completely still as if aping one of his taxidermized animals.

That memory grazed the edge of another, uncertain in Natalie's mind, something horrific she only thought she'd seen one night in a cemetery.

Both the memories and the figure downstairs made her shift on her feet. Could she retreat undetected? This stairway was no stranger to prey sensations, and she didn't want this apparition to catch her.

Below, a light rumbling slid from the seated figure.

Natalie clutched a hand over her heart. That was no ghost—her mother sat in one of the living room chairs, breath sliding in and out in an insect-like hum. She must have planned to keep Natalie from heading out tonight, but between work and mothering and her social life, sitting still in the dark was too tempting an invitation for sleep.

Natalie made a gentle descent, crossed the living room, and pulled her jacket off the coat rack. She reached for the front door and slid the locks with a careful hand, giving only the tiniest metallic *tick*.

Her mother's breath lifted into a light snore. With any luck, she would sleep through Natalie's absence and homecoming and never know the difference.

That would mean a long time sleeping in the chair. Natalie eased from the door, grabbed a blue-and-purple crochet blanket from the couch, and draped it over her sleeping mother. She looked almost peaceful.

Natalie smiled without meaning to and leaned down to kiss her mother's cheek.

Heather stirred beneath the blanket. "Nate?" she asked in a moaning whisper.

Natalie flinched to standing straight, yanked back by a claw in her heart. If there had been any doubt over her heading out tonight, it was gone. She didn't need *this*, she needed to feel—what? She wasn't sure which emotion mattered anymore.

Maybe it was that simple. She just needed to feel.

No more hesitating. Natalie headed out the door, closed it quietly behind her, and hurried for the driveway's end. Basil's truck arrived on time, and she smiled for him like she'd meant to, but she didn't kiss him now. A fidgety animal in her chest worried he might whisper-moan *Nate* like her mother had.

But Basil said nothing on the drive over. Maybe he'd used up every excuse and suggestion for keeping Natalie away from the Trip House. If he would only step inside with her, he would understand its beauty.

"You might like it," she said, sliding out of his passenger's seat and clutching her purse. "You might like doing something your parents wouldn't approve of."

Basil wrung his hands on the steering wheel. "See you in a few minutes."

That animal in Natalie's chest wanted to slam the truck door shut and shriek fury, but she would feel like shit then. She shut the door like usual, like a human being, and crossed the street.

Marty smiled when he saw her. Shane had puppy eyes. "We should give you a punch card," he said.

"Maybe next birthday," Natalie said, dropping her quarters into the pickle jar.

Its bottom looked sparse tonight, as did the leaf-dotted grass stretching between the sidewalk and the Trip House bricks. Kids seemed to be losing interest, choosing haunted house attractions elsewhere in town as October bled toward Halloween. They wanted a break from beauty.

Or maybe they were going into the Trip House and weren't coming out. Shane and Marty couldn't exactly enforce their time limits. They only wanted people to come out so they would have to pay to head back in. Repeat customers meant better business.

Maybe Natalie would stay longer this time. She might not come back at all.

She sank through the dark doorway where the Trip House pretended it had nothing to offer. Outside light brushed the edge of a concrete floor, but past that, there were no lights, no people, an illusion of nothingness.

Natalie was used to it now. She walked deeper into this threshold darkness. Every moment since her last visit had been a cold countdown to her return.

New light twinkled from inside, and her walk broke into a giddy run. Concrete gave way to gentle earth. The October chill cowered from a lovely warm night, and the only cold was the sense of two hands aiming their palms at her as if warming themselves over a campfire.

She didn't mind offering that heat. The Trip House had given her one warmth, and she could give another if only she would experience this softness and starlight.

If only she could be allowed to feel.

***

The phone rang once on Margaret's desk before cutting out. Trish must have answered it in the kitchen, and hopefully it wasn't the town hall archivist calling back. Margaret had tormented that poor young man enough with her questions about the pool house during a fruitless visit this afternoon. No town made a habit of confessing its sins.

Her desk was a disorderly mess of magnifying glasses, papers piled beneath the black rotary phone, a repair kit for her spectacle frames, a bendy-limbed lamp, among other odds and ends, but she kept the space clear around the audio adjuster. It was a broad gray box, similar to recording studio hardware but smaller and more limited. Margaret had popped open the cassette and mounted its eyes to spool their black tape through the device. She could slow it down, change output levels, and other tricks, all to pluck at soundscape secrets the world never wanted her to have.

Nothing emerged from the tape. No revelations caught at higher frequency, no whispers revealed at low volume, not even white noise. It was a tape of nothing.

A sudden knock startled Margaret in her seat. She hadn't noticed her office turning dark, and now its edges hugged her in a shadowy blanket.

Trish stood in the doorway, her fist lowering from the thick wooden door. A red coat hid her slender frame, and her brown face poked from beneath a violet hat meant for wintertime.

Margaret scowled. "You've been home, right?"

"Of course I've been home, love," Trish said. She dug mittens from her coat pockets. "But I'm heading out now."

Margaret glanced at her watch—past nine at night already. "Any special reason?"

"That was Gladys calling, hoping I'd visit the lads with her tonight. I agreed." Trish wrung her freshly mittened hands. "Arnie doesn't have long."

"Oh," Margaret said, an anvil dropping from her lips. "You shouldn't go alone."

Trish crossed the office with a smirk. "I won't be alone, remember? I'll be with Gladys, and we'll all play boardgames, and sing songs, and the nurse will tell us to keep it down, and we'll ignore her like always."

Margaret paused again. "But I should be with you."

"Tend the world your way, love," Trish said. "I'll tend it mine."

She bent beside Margaret's seat and kissed her cheek, then her lips, and then the tip of her nose, fogging Margaret's spectacles.

Margaret waited for Trish to leave before she wiped them on her blazer. From across the house, the front door jangled open with chimes and then clacked shut.

An airiness filled the office. Margaret sighed, half-expecting cloudy breath and fully expecting she wasn't alone, as if the lack of white noise on the tape was due to white noise having left the tape, and now it roamed her office, kissing silent footsteps to the floor, reaching its hands toward her.

She jerked toward the desk and glanced over her shoulder—nothing stood behind her. Same as there was nothing on the tape. Only memories of sound. Trish's footsteps. Margaret's sigh.

Ordinary life sounds, like earlier today.

"Wait a damn minute," Margaret snapped.

She scowled at the stretch of black tape. Her finger hunted the Rewind button on the audio adjuster and then hit Play again, at normal speed, normal levels. The playback should have sounded exactly as Margaret had recorded it this afternoon.

Silence, same as before.

Except silence didn't reflect the world she'd experienced. The microphone should have picked up the airy ambience within the pool house, the muffled cars beyond its walls, the crinkling of plastic sheets flapping in the wind, and Margaret's footsteps on tile flooring and concrete. Even if she'd forgotten to turn on the microphone, where was the hiss of an empty tape?

Nothing played from the machine's speaker. It was the suspicious quiet of misbehaving children. Too quiet.

Something had put effort into making sure Margaret picked up nothing amiss in the Trip House, but this was excessive nothing. A nothing untrue to life.

An overcorrection.

From the way Heather talked, Margaret had expected to find a smattering of kids wandering the grassy stretches between the street and the Trip House when she parked her car at the opposite curb. She only found a couple of college-aged kids pacing and smoking outside, fallen leaves crunching underfoot. Two boys right out of junior high braced the doorway in fold-out chairs. A larger boy in a letterman jacket sat behind the wheel of a red pickup truck, his elbows bracing the steering wheel, his fists against his forehead.

Margaret tapped his driver's window. "Are you Basil?"

The boy stared at her through the glass.

"Did you bring Natalie Glasgow here?" Margaret asked.

Gray eyes twitched to look past Margaret's shoulder and across the street.

To the Trip House. Of course. Margaret had hoped she could visit for reconnaissance and then return by daylight with one of her dwindling number of colleagues or at least a plan of approach, but now she needed to investigate tonight. This wouldn't be the first time Natalie had pushed a time limit.

Margaret patted the truck's door. "Go home. This isn't your problem anymore. I would steer clear of Natalie's house if I were you."

The boy recoiled, his broad frame pressing against his seat. Any suggestion of abandoning Natalie looked to offend him on a moral level—maybe even a religious ground—and Margaret wondered what kind of effect Natalie had on people besides her mother.

Margaret would find out soon. She crossed the street as Basil's truck pulled away, listening intently to her footsteps and getting a sense for them. They might not follow her into the Trip House.

One of the boys by the doorway lifted his head. "We got an age limit?"

"Money's money," the shorter boy said. "Dollar-fifty."

Margaret stormed past them, into the black emptiness, but she listened to their offended shouts and overdone adolescent cursing. The longer she kept grounded to the outside world, the better.

But she needed to touch the inside as well. "Natalie?" she called.

The Trip House darkness shut tight around her. It was almost substantive, a cloud of black vapor swelling against her limbs and torso, and then her face, eager to be breathed in, to breathe her in. A hazy quality swallowed her sense of direction. Which way to the plastic-sheeted windows? The front desk? The halls to the changing rooms? Margaret couldn't tell for certain, but she kept walking straight. The inner Trip House had become a liminal space, disconnected from the solid world, much like the smoke Margaret had used in clouding Nathaniel Glasgow's study years ago to draw out an invasive spirit.

Natalie might have been attracted more to these places of uncertainty than any spectral element of the world.

And yet there was something here, much as it liked to pretend otherwise.

"You wanted somewhere quiet," Margaret said. "But not somewhere lonely. The children could be your company, is that right?"

The darkness didn't answer, but her ear twitched at brushing air, an exasperated sigh beside her head. Silence had seeped through the building. No night sounds of insects clinging to life against the October chill, no angry boys shouting for their money.

"An interesting trick," Margaret said. "You made sure my recorder picked up nothing. It was too perfect. I should have heard my footsteps, the traffic outside. The air. Is the floor as clean as it looked this afternoon? Or are there holes in the walls, and you hid them from me? Is there garbage everywhere?" She stomped at her next step, forcing a concrete clack. "The trick seems easy for you now, at night. That must have taken a lot of effort in the daytime."

A voice like dry leaves and fine wine slid into her ear: "It was exhausting."

Margaret slowed her steps. To tease for an answer was one thing; to receive it was another. The illusions could have been the dreams of an empty building, but now she knew a presence inside the building had dredged up this darkness. Doubtful that was enough to entice Natalie and the other kids. This nothingness was a threshold between the outside and another experience. The true prize of the Trip House.

And what had Margaret discovered inside? She couldn't be sure, but it wasn't a ghost.

A stranger's breath crossed her ear, unsettling her hair. "Are you afraid?" he asked, eager to sound patient. "You don't have to be. No one comes to my heaven who doesn't want to. Even you."

Margaret forced her breathing to settle. The air was odorless. She should have detected autumn's decay, the pool house staleness, or her own sweat now dotting her forehead and the back of her neck. This illusion was an enforced nothingness.

Beyond it, she would find Natalie.

"Mine is a palace of kindness, where I keep a kind memory," the stranger said. "I am the finder of lost children, and the one you want—Natalie Glasgow? She was lost. Abandoned to circumstances she can't begin to understand."

Margaret bit her lower lip not to answer or explain. She had lured this creature into speaking, like he had lured Natalie inside. Best to let him speak.

"She loves her mother, that never changed." There was a smile in the stranger's voice. "But she's lonely and confused. I never wished to make her my possession. She longs to be taken. There is a fire in her unlike any I've felt before. Beyond human. She eases the cold."

Margaret took another halting step. She couldn't exactly call this the pool house anymore, or even the Trip House, though she was getting a sense for why the kids gave it that name. If only the darkness had a face for her to lock eyes with. This stranger preferred illusions, much like the kids who stepped inside. His *heaven*.

But there was a trade. A fire. An easing of cold.

Margaret's next step faltered as the air crawled from her neck. The stranger was inhaling her, an animal sniffing to understand.

"Mm," he hummed. "When were you last touched by a man? You were young and trembling, and he was older. I feel you speaking to him, and the terror at his discontent. Was he your father?"

Tension squeezed Margaret's neck and shoulders. She knew better than to look back, had kept herself from doing so many times before and likely saved her own life.

But she felt breath at her back, and she wanted to see how far she'd come from the doorway.

The outside was gone. No streetlights, no car headlights, as if the boys had draped the blanket onto its above-doorway nails again and sealed Margaret inside. If she tried to go back, there was no telling where she might end up. She could only keep moving.

No matter what she felt or heard.

Another inhalation brushed the back of her neck. "You feared abandonment. He put his hand on your shoulder and drew you close, and your trembling was over. Nothing to fear, until his heart or his lungs took him. In the end, he abandoned you after all."

Margaret reached ahead, hoping her fingers would tap the desk she'd seen in the afternoon. She would take slamming her hand into the wall and shooting an ache up her arm if she could only find a surface in the darkness.

"Answer. You chose to speak. Come closer, I can be your kindly touch." The stranger sighed along Margaret's arm. "A man's touch. I can even be your father, if you want it, alive even tonight. My heaven can be anything you like."

Margaret pursed her lips and took another step.

"It can even be a hell," the stranger said, turning severe. Harsher breath slithered in the thick air. "Rude animal, I can give you suffering."

A flicker of shape climbed from the corner of Margaret's sight, and again she couldn't keep her neck from twisting to look.

The darkness cut into the vague sense of another doorway—no, a hallway. To one of the changing rooms? Margaret didn't think so. She made out the scant semblance of a white linoleum floor beneath pale walls and fluorescent lighting, a hospital hallway. Moaning death reached for her from one of the rooms, growing fingers of sound.

She jerked back with a gasp and turned away.

The air forgot its odorless nature. There was a scent now, one Margaret almost didn't recognize, too many years had passed, but she vaguely recalled that rank plasticky burning smell mixed with fleshy rot. Another ghost-less house with a hole in its belly. She raised a hand to cover her mouth and nose.

Damp fingertips grazed her cheek, and she flung her arm down to look at her hand. Tangled tubing snaked over her fingers, red and heavy with death drawn from between another woman's legs.

"That was a decade ago," she whispered.

Her voice drowned in the dark as at last another sound snapped against her ears—an infant's pained cries.

Margaret closed her eyes and took another step. She put her weight into it, grinding against the concrete and joining its sound with the infant's cry. Tugging her loose from memory.

Didn't the stranger know? A stillborn infant couldn't make a sound. Crying at a birth site was a good sign; it said the baby was alive. Margaret wished she'd heard a cry that day, with that woman's blood coating her arms.

The stranger had made another overcorrection. Had he never slid his hands into the wet messiness of birth, expecting to find life but instead cradling death? Of course not. He couldn't understand.

Margaret thought back to the first time she'd fallen into an illusion. She had stood in a grave, covered in soil and sweat, where she lost her consciousness in the memories of a golden-haired beast with massive claws. Margaret had lost her thoughts to it, too. For a moment, they had been one creature, one spirit.

She remembered leaving that vision, too. Rising from it had been a jarring instant, snapping from grasslands heat to a cool autumn night, reinhabiting her upright posture, human arms and legs, and un-animal thoughts. She remembered recapturing the here and now.

And she could do it again.

Fingers, toes, arms, legs, heartbeat, thinking, entered this house, darkness, seeking.

A pinprick of light broke the ceiling above. Another shined beside it, and then another. The black cloud ebbed little by little.

Margaret took her next step, and her sole crunched crisp blades of grass.

"Natalie struggles in your world," the stranger said. "Ten minutes out there is not a crumb of the feast of time she needs in my gentle sanctuary. Each goodbye nearly tears her apart. She doesn't belong in her mother's house of sorrows. She belongs in my meadow."

Margaret could see it now—wild grass stroked her legs, gentle as Trish's hands, and brilliant starlight shined across a cloudless blue-black sky. Distant dark mountains broke apart the sweeping cosmos and loomed over a sloping meadow that spread into lazy hills. Scattered maple trees grasped the rich black earth with thick roots, overgrown by lush violet flowers. Giggling shadows roamed the landscape, their jackets flapping in the calm breeze.

There was Natalie, her cloud of lion-gold hair unmistakable. She had her mother's lips, her father's nose, and eyes of wildfire. Small wonder the stranger had been drawn to her and chosen to draw her in. She ran a circle around an indistinct cluster of other figures, other kids, some kind of game, and each of them sang with laughter.

The stranger's voice drifted on the wind. "Now you see my meadow. Your eyes may behold a forever starlight."

Margaret studied the distance between herself and Natalie. Ten yards? Twelve? Margaret didn't have Natalie's long legs, but she could charge like a train engine, cross the grass, grab Natalie's arm, and haul her back before the stranger could mine another tragic memory from Margaret's thoughts.

But haul Natalie where? The meadow stretched in every direction as if poured into a bowl-shaped mountain range.

The stranger sighed into the wind. "Do you know the sensation of having no choice but to leave home? I hunted north of this place until others hunted me in turn, harmed me. But here I found a forgotten hollow, a nothing, a sanctuary to *become* nothing until I healed."

North—did he mean Maine? Canada? The Arctic? Margaret couldn't be sure, but she was getting an idea for what she might have encountered here. Legends sometimes walked the world. Or crawled if they had been beaten to the ground and presumed dead.

Margaret bent toward the grass and ran her hands over the velvet-soft blades. Small round pebbles dotted the soil around fallen maple branches.

"I was overburdened," the stranger went on. "To travel, to be nothing, I had to lose pieces of myself. Shedding friends and lovers and enemies, that was simple. Memories don't want to leave. Worse, we're reluctant to force them out."

Margaret shifted on her haunches—a new sensation had crept into the air, disguised by the stranger's voice, a sense of splayed hands hovering over her as if she were a campfire on a chilly night. A cold skin dressed the wind, needing warmth.

The stranger was close.

"But I did shed the memories," he said. "Tore them to harmless fragments—all but one. I had to keep this one. A sacred memory. How was I to know my heaven would draw the lost?"

Margaret shuddered. He talked the sanctity of memories when he'd tried to use hers against her? What would he have done to Natalie if she'd chosen to defy him?

And what was he doing to her now?

Out on the grass, Natalie kept running her circles, but the nearby figures swayed with the wind. They might have been flesh and bone once, but now they looked like standing shadows cast by flickering flames. Natalie might be flickering, too, a fire forgetting how to stay alight.

What remained of lost children when all their heat wore out? The truth burned into Margaret's skull—Natalie, encircling shadows.

Natalie, becoming a shadow.

This could not go on. Violence was not the right way to break or cast out a spirit. Not for experts like Margaret, more for amateurs and cowards.

But what choice did she have?

She patted at the grass and tightened her fist around a stiff maple branch. Her other hand splayed into the breeze, sliding through her fingers like tongues of air eager to taste her—closer to the truth than anything else the stranger had shown her tonight. If seeing was not believing, she would have to feel.

"A lure is not the fisher." The stranger's voice turned prideful. "No one lurked with a beckoning finger. This should have been a lonesome crawl of time. Do you understand? I didn't seek out the lost—they found me. They mistook this place for recreation until they awakened me, and once I understood them, I took away the hollow and offered them the meadow, *my* meadow, the refuge of an ancient soul who long ago wore out his welcome back home."

Margaret stood up and pawed at the wind. Her fingers clenched and spread. One heel ground against the grass, searching for the concrete truth underneath.

"The desperate will always seek a beautiful peace," the stranger said. "My memory lives again, filled by the needful. I am their bringer of blessings. I give them heaven, I give them love. What would you give them?"

Margaret shut her eyes again and thought of a lion's vision, a memory like this one, and the sense of emerging from that memory. Coming up from underwater. Having her own experiences and thoughts and the here and now. This stranger believed he'd brought love in his hunger, but Margaret had seen through a predator's eyes before. She only needed to break through this one's illusion.

Limbs, heartbeat, body, senses, thought—there.

Her hand rested on an unseen shoulder of ragged cloth and frail bone.

"Nothing then. The lost inherit nothing." The windy stranger trembled, little more than a skeleton. "So, you are the one who kills heaven."

Margaret gritted her teeth and thrust the maple branch forward.

Its firm end pierced a muddy breastbone, where a once-solid ribcage and sternum had decayed to skin-like frailty. Empty air shaped soppy shadows around a fleshy skull, shrieking and gasping and choking as its body tried to jerk away from Margaret, but her piercing branch held it in place.

A silver crown gleamed in the starlight as it slid from the stranger's head. It fell toward the grass and soil, but the impact sounded like metal against concrete, a silver coin on a pool house floor. Skeletal hands splayed around Margaret, greedy and cold, but she forced the branch deeper. Bony fingers grasped at the air as if she were the illusion.

Perhaps the stranger was so lost to time that he had forgotten the minor details of life and humanity, only seeing his meadow. He'd chosen to drown in his treasured memory.

But Margaret had to fill that pool with concrete truth. She yanked the branch out, tearing a black sucking hole into the air.

Screams broke across the meadow and echoed against the mountain range. The night sky yanked downward like a curtain caught in the mouth of a gargantuan vacuum cleaner, and the hills and grass chased after it, this world turning to rainwater as it spilled down a gutter. The trees, the flowers—everything swirled toward the emptiness.

Even the other people. Thin shadows flitted past, weightless and bodiless, their laughing forms now screeching in the wind. Margaret ducked under them and charged for Natalie.

She was losing her balance, maybe caught between sinking into shadow and memory versus living in the real world beyond. Her wild eyes turned to Margaret, and her jacket rippled with the sucking wind.

Fingers, toes, arms, legs.

Margaret closed her hand around Natalie's forearm and tugged her close. They lurched together, but Margaret stiffened in place.

Heartbeat, thinking, entered this house, darkness, seeking.

"It isn't real!" Margaret shouted. The illusion tore into howling emptiness around them. "It can't kill you, Natalie! It isn't real, but you still are!"

Natalie couldn't see. Her eyes were open wide like they'd forgotten how to blink, but now burly arms grasped her head and pressed her to a soft chest, hiding her face against a thick shirt. She could only hear panic and fear in the wind while a cold brass button dug into her cheek. This woman hugging her didn't want her to see the tumult around them, had kept her from seeing another horror in the past, and though Natalie couldn't entirely remember that night, her body must have. It settled into the embrace, knowing better than to fight out of it until the monstrous screaming at last went quiet.

A hand eased from the back of Natalie's head, sliding its fingers out of her hair. An arm lifted from her shoulders. She drew up but not away, not yet ready to step back, and looked around for the starlit meadow.

She tried to remember peacefulness. Hadn't she felt it? Clearly, unavoidably, as if calm were a liquid feeling injected into her blood.

But the illusion was gone. The Trip House had offered a lie, and much as she'd enjoyed that lie, she couldn't trick herself into feeling it was truth again. There were no other kids left here. Only cold hands and shadowy memories had joined her in the meadow. Only a laughter that was really screaming.

The gloom inside the pool house hunched around her now. Her sneakers scraped the floor, where a shaft of broken wood lay beside the woman's shoes. Shattered glass sprinkled the concrete nearby, while dead leaves, soda cans, filthy plastic shopping bags, cigarette butts, and other trash littered the floor where it met the wall, most of it coated in dust. No one had added to the refuse in some time. Dark crevices mottled the walls, most of them blanketed with cobwebs.

Natalie hadn't imagined the true inside would look this dirty and worn.

A chilly breath stroked her shoulders, and she clutched against the woman, her back to another wall. Maybe another timeworn opening, too.

"You shouldn't look," the woman said.

She was shorter and older than Natalie's mother by a few years, with a thickset frame. The faint light through the plastic-sheeted windows glowed against a round, gentle face and reflected in her spectacles.

Natalie pivoted to face the wall, and then she flinched away, pressing her back against the woman's chest. Clammy hands closed on her shoulders and kept her from falling over.

A slender crack opened at a corner where one changing room met a hallway leading from the pool house entrance. Within the crumbling plaster, a wooden support beam jutted alongside a narrow husk, staring out with empty skull sockets, lengthy fingers curling at its chest, and large sharp teeth gleaming like Natalie would have expected in a lion's mouth.

Her ears twitched at a brief thump, almost a heartbeat. Something had crawled inside these broken walls long after the pool house shut down. An almost alive something.

But she heard nothing else inside it. One thump, a heart giving out mid-pump, and then the husk crumbled over the plaster. Only another black crevice stared from the pool house wall.

Natalie shuddered beneath the woman's hands and turned back to her. "He wasn't what he told me, was he?" Except she couldn't be certain what she'd been told anymore.

"No," the woman said. "Natalie, I'm Margaret Willow. Do you remember me?"

Fragments of recognition flaked through Natalie's thoughts. They never formed a perfect picture, but maybe real memories were imperfect. A pretend one, like a meadow full of laughter—that was easy, like drawing it on a page.

The truth was harder. Time ate holes into it, and anyone who wanted to remember it could only do their best to nod at this strange woman in the dark and hope that was enough.

Margaret closed a gentle hand around Natalie's arm. "I'm taking you home."

Natalie hugged her free arm around herself and nodded again. She'd missed a crucial element of her time here, of every visit to the Trip House, but she had a feeling the trip was wrong. A part of her wondered if the trip was really hers. More likely it belonged to that thing in the wall, and she was the vehicle.

Margaret led the way outside, where Shane and Marty started shouting together.

"You didn't pay!"

"That was way too long!"

Natalie pawed to reach for her purse, but it was gone. She must have dropped it in the meadow, and it had been swallowed by the broken illusion, same as the people who'd faded into shadows. That didn't sound possible, but she didn't have another explanation.

Margaret wheeled around on Shane and Marty. "Both of you little boys had better clear out of here before I find some real trouble to put you in."

She didn't wait to see what either of them would do; their shutting up must've been good enough for her. She led across the grass and street, her fingers still encircling Natalie's arm. Basil's pickup truck was gone. Margaret must have told him to clear out, too, and he was too much of an obedient follower to dare argue. A small, boxy car waited at the curb.

Natalie climbed into the passenger's seat and hung her head. Margaret filled the driver's seat beside her. She expected to hear a key slam into the ignition, for the car to rumble alive, and then they would drive back to her mother's house. To home.

But Margaret deflated against her seat, pressing both hands to the steering wheel. "You and I need to break this habit," she said. "Try seeing each other when your life isn't in danger."

Natalie kept her head down. "What did it want?" She could hardly manage above a defeated whisper.

"What most people want," Margaret said. "Food. Company. A sense they're doing a good thing for someone else so they can feel good about themselves, which gives them the right to hurt other people, too. He was cold inside, but he'd found something to warm him. And he didn't care if there was fire left afterward." Her knuckles whitened as she gripped the steering wheel. "He would've done it to you."

"It was easier," Natalie said. "In there."

Margaret gave a slow nod and then at last slid the key into the ignition. "I know. He probably thought so, too." The car rumbled alive. "It's alright to cry. I've seen you cry before."

Natalie's hand snapped to Margaret's. "Don't tell Mom. Please."

"You're not in trouble," Margaret said. "She'll be happy to know you're safe."

"I don't care about that," Natalie said. "If she hears what really happened, she'll be scared again. And I don't want to scare her anymore."

Margaret's expression crumpled. She opened her mouth like she meant to give Natalie a lecture about lying, or to tell her she couldn't help scaring her mother. It was the kind of look her father used to give when he found she'd vacuumed without being asked or took an interest in the prizes he brought home from abroad, moments when he called her a young lady. Maybe to Margaret, Natalie had sounded adult.

But she wasn't interested in praise. Her mother couldn't go through anything like the hell of recovering from slash wounds in her gut while fretting over Natalie's well-being. Heather didn't deserve it, and Natalie was tired of putting the people she loved through the trouble.

"Alright," Margaret said at last. "You were drinking with boys from your school. No, college freshmen. You should've known better. She'll ground you for it, but she won't be scared of anything strange. Only that you're growing up."

Natalie sat still, absorbing this, and then blinked at Margaret. "Okay."

Margaret reached for Natalie's face and lifted her chin. "She really left her mark, didn't she? Like pawprints in the earth."

"Is that normal?" Natalie asked.

"I've never seen another case quite like yours before," Margaret said, drawing her hand back. "No, it isn't normal. And I suppose if you're going to keep stumbling into bizarre circumstances, we should spend more time together. Catch you up on a little of what I know about the world." She flashed a gentle smile. "Your mother would have fewer reasons to be afraid for you."

"And me?" Natalie fixed desperate eyes on Margaret. "Would it be normal for me?"

"Never." Margaret adjusted her spectacles. "I've told this to your mother and many others in the past—you're never desensitized to the strange, Natalie. What's scary once will be scary again, and there's always something new. And you might be different each time, and afraid in a unique way, and even in danger, which will never feel right or sane. But you can be prepared."

Natalie eased into her seat. She let her muscles hang around her bones and only moved to obey Margaret's command of putting on her seatbelt.

The road slid beneath the car as it shifted from the curb. Streetlights swept to either side of the windshield and flashed through the passenger window across Natalie's face. She patted her fingers along her jaw, her cheeks, feeling for large sharp teeth like that thing in the Trip House wall. Like a lioness.

A golden hair caught between her fingers. Snared in the way she'd caught a little of the animal inside her years ago. Had she torn away some of that creature with its heavenly meadow, too?

If so, she wanted to believe she'd stolen the pleasant lie. She wanted to believe she wasn't shellshocked by losing the meadow but instead had inherited a transcendent calm, stronger than the real thing. Better to believe that than to think she might've borrowed its parasitic needs or its selfish delusions. She was enough trouble for the people around her already.

And she wondered if her father had felt the world catching on him. Spirits here, animals there, never understanding any of it and so choosing destruction.

She could never know for certain. She could only prepare. Ghosts lay behind her—her father, her possessor, the kind-voiced creature in the Trip House. And if Margaret told it right, more ghosts waited ahead.

A ghostland for Natalie Glasgow.

AFTERWORD

(from *Of Night Tyrants and Terrors*)

I couldn't shake wanting to write about someone possessed by an animal's ghost, specifically a lioness. Shaping this in an exorcism narrative only seemed natural.

Still, without a demon, what good would priests do for Natalie? I wanted an exorcism that followed the roads of witchcraft and with some understanding for the possessor rather than dominance and clashing wills.

The Christian God sits this one out, leaving only Mother Nature, and in her immediacy, she is terrifying, unpredictable, and far harder to please. I didn't want to tell a story about vengeance, but about pain and heartache, and how those troubles make us lash out, whether we're witches or housewives, children or predators.

Tom Waits sang that the Earth died screaming, but it also dies clawing and biting and furious.

ABOUT THE AUTHOR

Hailey Piper is a Bram Stoker Award-winning author whose books include *Queen of Teeth* from Strangehouse Books, as well as *A Light Most Hateful, No Gods for Drowning, The Worm and His Kings* trilogy, and other books of dark fiction. She is an active member of the Horror Writers Association, with over a hundred short stories appearing in *Weird Tales, Pseudopod, Cosmic Horror Monthly*, and other publications. She lives with her wife in Maryland, where their occult rituals are secret.

Find Hailey at www.haileypiper.com